A VOICE FROM BEYOND

The medium rested her head back, eyes closed, and a veil of silence fell over the room. Darnell could not see well in the dim light. He focused his attention on the medium, only glancing at the others. Soon, he heard her give out a soft, slight moan in a quavering voice. He waited.

The voice slowly grew in intensity. The sound stopped, and the medium now spoke in a high-pitched female voice.

Darnell was astonished to hear that the sound was totally unlike the medium's own voice. The tone suggested the still-girlish speech of a young woman.

"Mother . . . Mother . . ." the voice came.

Margaret gasped with a sharp intake of breath. "It's Mair!"

"You must find Megan, protect her . . . bombs . . . destruction from the skies, fire, smoke, shining lights . . . death . . ."

Darnell hung on every word, searching for a trace of the medium's own voice, not knowing Mair's voice. He was amazed at what he heard, but thought whatever it was it couldn't be true.

At that instant the red light above them went out, plunging the room into complete darkness. A chorus of cries and groans came from around the table, and Lloyd George's wife shrieked. . . .

Also by Sam McCarver

The Case of Cabin 13
The Case of Compartment 7
The Case of the 5th Victim *

* Coming in 2001

THE CASE OF THE 2ND SÉANCE

A JOHN DARNELL MYSTERY

Sam McCarver

A SIGNET BOOK

SIGNET
Published by New American Library, a division of
Penguin Putnam Inc., 375 Hudson Street,
New York, New York 10014, U.S.A.
Penguin Books Ltd, 27 Wrights Lane,
London W8 5TZ, England
Penguin Books Australia Ltd, Ringwood,
Victoria, Australia
Penguin Books Canada Ltd, 10 Alcorn Avenue,
Toronto, Ontario, Canada M4V 3B2
Penguin Books (N.Z.) Ltd, 182–190 Wairau Road,
Auckland 10, New Zealand

Penguin Books Ltd, Registered Offices:
Harmondsworth, Middlesex, England

First published by Signet, an imprint of New American Library,
a division of Penguin Putnam Inc.

First Printing, November 2000
10 9 8 7 6 5 4 3 2 1

 REGISTERED TRADEMARK—MARCA REGISTRADA

Printed in the United States of America

For Ginger

ACKNOWLEDGMENTS

Sherlock Holmes, called the greatest detective in the annals of fiction, and thought by millions to be real and perhaps even still alive, received his immortal literary life from his creator, Arthur Conan Doyle—Sir or Dr., as you wish. I thank Conan Doyle for that eternal service to us mystery readers and writers, and I pay homage to him in this book as he assists Professor John Darnell in his investigations. This is an echo of the good doctor's own successful investigations of real crimes during his lifetime. Doyle, and other real-life persons—not the least of whom is David Lloyd George, Prime Minister of England at the time this story takes place—are included in the tale told in my book. However, except for their involvement in historical and documented events, their participation in this story derives from my imagination, since this book is a work of fiction.

I thank Joseph Pittman, Senior Editor of New American Library, for his advice, perceptive editorial reviews, enthusiasm, and support. I'm thankful for NAL's excellent copy-editors and their indispensable reviews, and NAL's cover design artists, and their classic and compelling covers. And I'm grateful to my literary agent, Donald Maass, for his encouragement and literary guidance.

Chapter 1

London. Thursday, December 14, 1916

In the darkened room, the seven faces around the table took on an otherworldly glow in the diffused, red light of the beaded chandelier overhead. The lamp's dim, blood-red bulb cast devilish shadows downward upon their faces, suggesting a scene of hellishness in the eerie gloom. Pouring rain outside added a fitting setting for the séance. Warned by the medium that if the circle was broken the power of the séance itself would be destroyed, the seven held each other's hands tightly.

The strong right hand of Prime Minister David Lloyd George held the silky, smooth left hand of his wife, Margaret. She held her daughter's hand on her right, occasionally squeezing it to reassure her. Their daughter, Megan, fourteen, allowed her hand to rest gently in the moist grip of Sir Arthur Conan Doyle. On his right Doyle clasped in his own gnarled fingers the hand of Robert Brent, the Prime Minister's young private secretary.

Brent, in turn, lay his manicured hand in that of the minister's personal cabinet aide, Hugo Stanton, who gripped the spidery hand of Madame Ilena Ispenska, the medium. She completed the circle of seven by resting her hand unctuously in the left hand of the Prime Minister.

"Shall we begin?" David Lloyd George's ordinarily smooth voice cut the silence with a sharp edge as he glared into the black eyes of the medium. Her reticence and imperious air bothered him. She'd said less than a dozen words since her arrival, seeming to enjoy engendering a cloak of mystery about her work. Lloyd George had accepted her after his aides interviewed her, and Conan Doyle assured him that if anyone could achieve spirit contact, she could. It was too late to turn back now.

"We begin." The medium tossed her long, gray-streaked brown hair backward as she leaned her head on the chair rim and closed her eyes. "Absolute silence," she commanded, in a thick accent. "Do not speak, no matter what you hear or see. Much time, this may take."

To Lloyd George, the grimly lit room at Number Ten Downing Street in London seemed a lifetime away from that bleak night in 1907 almost exactly nine years earlier when his daughter Mair died from illness in the bloom of her youth, at age seventeen. The anniversary of her death just two weeks earlier had brought the usual renewed dreams in which she came to him each year, with arms outstretched in supplication. This year, the dreams and his reaction were more intense.

Mair's death took the joy out of Lloyd George's comfortable life, and he felt continuing guilt for losing her. He berated himself at her death—*Couldn't he have found better doctors? Should he have spent more time with her, brought her to London more often, despite the demands of his position? Was her death punishment for his affairs with Catherine Davies and other younger women?* For nine years, the nagging thoughts tore at his psyche and denied him peace.

Sitting in the darkened room now, waiting for some sign from the medium, Lloyd George thought back on his struggles to obtain relief after his daughter's death. He remembered Mair's funeral, how he tried for release, talking it out afterward, in a six-mile walk with friends, trying somehow to expiate his guilt.

He glanced sidelong at his wife, Maggie, who had supported him strongly over the years, submerging her own grief and her suffering from his romantic extramarital affairs. Her hair was graying, yet a sparkle and strength could still flash from her green eyes. He knew how much she'd helped him while his star rose in England's political sky, and he still relied upon her.

Now Mair's image, a ghostly likeness, flashed in his mind anew this night. He remembered how, the first time he began to relive Mair's death, he'd confided tearfully to Maggie, "Little Mair came to me in a dream."

Since that first dream, his grief had been renewed in many dreams of her, always beginning on the anniversary of her death, November 30. He knew it was becoming an obsession. Burdened by World War I battles and losses for two years, he was desperate now to escape from those dark memories.

Lloyd George's thoughts swirled in the silence and darkness of the room. He squinted at Conan Doyle's bulky shape in the dim light and wondered what the writer was thinking just then. Was he still confident of success in this bizarre experiment he had urged for several years, and to which Lloyd George had yielded at last, this year?

After Lloyd George's elevation to Prime Minister and the move to Ten Downing Street, a week earlier, the dreams were severe, and Doyle pressed him again. "Hold a séance, David. In your dreams, Mair is saying she needs to talk with you. You believe in an afterlife, a spiritual world, so you should believe in a way to reach those who have passed on. A medium might reach Mair. She could help you through your dark tunnel of grief."

"She?"

"Mediums are almost all women. They seem to have the knack for it. They're more sensitive, and have more of a sixth sense, more extrasensory perception."

"I don't know . . . A séance sounds so strange. Will the medium sound horns, move things about, levitate tables? I've heard stories about eerie things you see and hear."

Doyle shook his head. "There'll be no materializations of strange objects out of thin air. And no ectoplasm."

"No . . . what?"

"Ectoplasm. Spirit images in a physical form flowing from the medium. The stuff ghosts are made of. None of that fakery."

"Thank God. My heart couldn't take it."

"You'll just hear Mair send you a message from the spirit world, speaking through the medium's voice."

Lloyd George had taken his wife's hand in his that night and looked into her eyes for guidance. "What do you think, Maggie?"

She smiled. "David, if it will make you happy . . ."

"We could talk with Mair. The dreams could stop."

His wife said, "Yes . . . perhaps."

Lloyd George had reluctantly agreed, musing, "The House of Commons will be adjourned until the nineteenth." At last, with eyes moist and glistening, he decided. "We'll try it. We'll reach our daughter. I know we will. I can feel it."

Now he glanced about the table, barely able to see the eyes of those sitting there. The eyes of the medium on his one side were shut tight, he could see that, and his wife's, on his other side, were also closed. As for the rest of them, it was too dark to see.

Madame Ispenska sat rigidly, her head back, a slight moan coming from her parted lips. Lloyd George continued to worry because he knew little about her. He nursed misgivings, still, about the séance, and felt almost foolish. Yet if he could hear one word from Mair, it would be worth all the bizarre routines and humiliation spiritualism required. The medium claimed her séances allowed her to reach soldiers killed in the war. And Doyle would not call it impossible, and evidently believed it.

Lloyd George's secretary, Brent, opposite him, sat with his head held down to his chest. His aide, Stanton, was unmoving. His daughter, Megan, next to his wife, was also silent and motionless. Doyle sat straight, stiffly, chin jutting forward. In the dimness, that was all Lloyd George could see. He closed his own eyes and took a deep breath.

He felt the medium's hand tighten in his. She seemed to be going into a trance. Doyle had said this would happen, and, in the trance, she could contact Mair, who would speak through her. Now, hearing Madame Ispenska's moans grow louder, Lloyd George hoped he'd soon hear Mair's words.

The medium jerked back and stiffened. Her grip felt like steel, and her voice rose from the low moan to a harsh shriek. Suddenly the overhead light went out, and the room was plunged into pitch-black darkness. Chairs scraped back on the hardwood floor and hands dropped their tight grips on one another.

"Dammit!" the Prime Minister shouted. "Fix these blasted lights, somebody."

He rose, seeing nothing, and groped his way by instinct toward the hall door. He stumbled against his secretary, who uttered an exclamation as he banged against the open hall door. The hallway, equally dark, emitted no light into the room.

"The whole house is without electricity," Brent said. "I'll check the fittings in the cellar. Stay here, sir." His cautious footsteps proceeded down the hall.

"There's a candle in the sideboard drawer, David," Lloyd George's wife called, "if you can get to it . . ."

"No matches," he answered her, and worked his way back to his chair. He ran his hands through his hair and sat still.

Madame Ispenska moaned again, and Lloyd George heard her voice ask, "What . . . what happened?"

"Don't get up," he said. "The lights went out."

"Oh, my head. The trance—it was to begin." She groaned. "My head aches. This is not good."

"Everyone stay in your seats," Lloyd George called

to the others. "Don't move about in the dark. We'll have light soon."

Conan Doyle's deep Scotch brogue boomed throughout the room. "This never happens in a séance. Be cautious, David."

The voices seemed sepulchral in the dark. Lloyd George said, "It's our damned London electricity problem, that's all."

At his words, the lights flicked on, white lights in the hallway, the red light overhead. The group breathed a collective sigh. Stanton and Brent reentered the room.

"I think it'll hold, now," Brent said, dusting his hands.

"Good. Shall we try again, Madame Ispenska?" The Prime Minister glanced at his wife, who looked calm, then back at the medium.

"I try. Take seats, please. We see." She took her seat and stretched an arm out in each direction, her hands open, to grasp the others' hands.

"Megan's not here," the Prime Minister's wife remarked to her husband. "She probably went to her room."

Lloyd George looked at Megan's vacant chair and frowned. "We shouldn't have put her through it, Maggie. She'll have nightmares."

"But she wanted to hear Mair's voice, too. I should talk with her," his wife said, standing and looking at her husband.

"We must begin," the medium announced, closing her eyes as if to punctuate her comment.

Lloyd George's wife took her seat, with a sigh, saying to her husband, "Well, I'll look in on her when we finish, then."

The participants all grasped hands again in the circle around the table. The hubbub settled down into abject silence, broken only by the audible heavy breathing of Conan Doyle.

Minutes stretched into a half hour. The medium continued to sit back in her chair, eyes closed, but no sound came from her lips, none of the light moan that earlier seemed to be the beginning of a trance. Finally she said, "No use. My contact was interrupted. We try again another time." She dropped the Prime Minister's hand and stood. "I am exhausted. I go now."

"Sorry, David," Doyle said, coming over to the Prime Minister. He frowned as he took Lloyd George's hand in both of his. "Next time, we'll have better luck."

"I hope so. We must keep trying."

Brent inserted a white light overhead, replacing the red bulb the medium had insisted be installed before the séance. Stanton, Doyle, and Madame Ispenska said their good nights to Lloyd George and his wife.

Talking softly, the three walked to the front door, out to the street, and called for their motorcars to be brought around for them.

Inside, Brent told Lloyd George, "I have to stop by your office for a few minutes, sir. I need to get your papers in order for your War Cabinet meeting tomorrow."

Lloyd George nodded. "All right, Robert. Let yourself out when you're finished."

He and his wife walked, hand in hand, up the stairs to the bedroom level. Margaret said, "I'll just say good night to Megan," and stopped at her daughter's bedroom door.

Lloyd George patted her on the arm and continued trudging toward their bedroom, his head low, lips tight, eyes moist. He thrust his hands deep into his pockets, a habit he'd formed in his schoolboy days, when depressed. The failed experiment had raised his hopes to the sky and then dashed them to the ground.

His wife stepped back out into the hallway from the bedroom and called to him, "She's not here, dear. Megan's not here."

Lloyd George heard the concern in her voice and turned to walk back toward her. "What? Not there?"

"Not in her room."

"Maybe she's down in the kitchen," he said, speaking as he returned to his wife's side. "She likes her milk and biscuits before bed."

She brightened. "Oh yes. We must go and see."

They wound their way down the stairways to the kitchen, where the cook was preparing meat for the next day. "Was Megan here, Mrs. Beecher?" Lloyd George asked.

"No, sir. I wondered . . ."

Lloyd George cut her off, anxious now, saying, "Come with me, Maggie." He took his wife's hand and they hurried up to his reception office on the main floor.

Brent sat at a table, working on papers. He looked up, raising his eyebrows, as they entered the room.

"Megan's missing!" Lloyd George said to him. "Help us search for her."

Brent dropped his pen and came to Lloyd George's side.

"You take the lower floors, Robert," Lloyd George urged, "and Maggie and I'll go to the upper ones. Come back down here to the hall when you finish."

The three rushed off, Brent in one direction, the Prime Minister and his wife to his private study, where Megan often came during the day, thinking she might be asleep on one of the couches. "Megan, Megan!" he called out, his voice echoing off the wooden beams of the empty room.

His wife looked into Megan's room again, then they hurried on to their bedroom, hoping Megan was waiting there for them, perhaps asleep on their bed, but that was also fruitless. They rushed from room to room throughout the upper floors, Lloyd George getting more concerned each minute. When every room had been checked, he and Margaret returned to the lower hallway, where they found Brent.

"I checked outside, sir," he said breathlessly, "and with the doorman. No one saw her leave the front. I looked through the garden in back, and found no trace of her going out there. The French doors to it were locked."

The now-frantic Lloyd George stared at him with red-streaked eyes. "I need Conan Doyle here. He's staying at the Ritz, Robert. Bring him back here, as fast as you can."

"Yes, sir." The secretary dashed out into the rainy night, shouting for the garage attendant to bring a motorcar around.

"Let's wait in the living room," Lloyd George said to his wife, and took her into the great room where they sat side by side, holding hands, on a sofa.

Margaret's eyes overflowed with tears as she sobbed, "Oh, David. Where's our Megan? She's never gone off like this."

Lloyd George said, "There must be some explanation. She has to turn up. We lost one daughter—we can't lose another. That would kill me, Maggie."

Twenty minutes later, Brent burst into the living room with a harried-looking Conan Doyle striding after him, Doyle's tie loose and collar unbuttoned, his coat moist from the rain.

Doyle said to Lloyd George, "Robert told me about Megan. How can I help?"

Lloyd George grabbed Doyle's lapels. "I need to know one thing, Arthur." His voice cracked as he asked, "Could she have been drawn into the spirit world?"

His wife looked at her husband with wild eyes. "Spirit world, David? My God."

"I don't know, dear. I'm just asking." He stared up at Doyle. "Well, Arthur? What do you say, man? Is it possible? Could spirits have taken her?"

Doyle gripped the Prime Minister's shoulder. "I don't know what to make of it . . . Nothing like this has ever happened in any séance I've known of."

Lloyd George said, "That damned medium. Who can help us? There must be someone." Lloyd George paced back and forth. "You know about this spiritualism business, Arthur."

Margaret broke down, crying. Her high voice wailed.

"Please do something, somebody. I want my little girl back."

Lloyd George sat and put his arm around her. She leaned her head against his chest and continued sobbing. After a few moments, she stopped and stared blankly, straight ahead.

Lloyd George looked up at Doyle. "Arthur?"

Doyle frowned and pulled at his plentiful mustache. "There's Scotland Yard, of course . . ."

Lloyd George burst out, "No, no. The news would leak out. The new Prime Minister involved in a séance? In the middle of a war? The press would make a laughing stock of me. I can't lose the trust of the people." He stood and resumed his pacing.

Margaret frowned, and stared at him as he moved back and forth. "David . . . ," she said, but stopped.

Doyle tugged at his mustache again. "I know someone who investigates matters of the occult, the spirit world, and psychic phenomena. He can look into this for you confidentially. Professor John Darnell."

Lloyd George's forehead creased. "Darnell? Oh yes . . . the *Titanic* tragedy."

"He calls himself a psychichologist, a debunker of the supernatural. He teaches psychology and philosophy. He's investigated and dealt with spirit sightings and many apparent paranormal events. You may remember the Leeds Castle case. Ghosts reported there."

"Yes. Then get him. Now, tonight. Tell him I demand it."

"No need for pressure, David. I've known Darnell for years. He's my friend. I'll have him here in an hour if he's in town."

Conan Doyle took Lloyd George's hand in his. "Hold firm, David." He said to Margaret, "We'll find your daughter, Maggie. No matter what it takes."

Doyle turned to Brent, who stood listening, openmouthed. "Drive me to Darnell's flat, Robert. And let's use your fastest car this time. Every minute counts."

Chapter 2

Thursday midnight, December 14, 1916

The steward pounded on the door of cabin 13. "The *Titanic*'s going down! We're sinking . . . Come to the door, John." Who was calling him John? A steward? Darnell couldn't place the voice. He couldn't wake, couldn't shake off the feeling that he was, somehow, on board the ill-fated ship again.

His eyes blinked open. He heard the words clearly now through his open window, a familiar gruff voice coming from the street. "John! Come to the door, John!" He rubbed his eyes, and pushed long, vagrant strands of hair back from his forehead.

His wife, Penny, turned to him. Sleep in her eyes, she stifled a yawn and placed a hand on his arm. "Who's shouting at the front door? It must be nearly midnight."

Darnell threw back the covers and stumbled to the window. He peered down at the two men huddled on his front stoop in the rain, and called, "Who is it?"

The taller one, a heavily built man, removed his bowler hat and looked up. In the streetlight, Darnell saw the man's face now, and told Penny over his shoulder, "It's Conan Doyle." He called out the window, "I'll be right there, Arthur."

Darnell grabbed a robe and pulled open the door to the hallway. He rushed down the stairs two at a time and crossed the entryway to the front door with long strides.

His valet, Sung, hurried from his servants' quarters on the ground floor. "Do you need me, sir?" Sung asked, seeing Darnell at the front door.

"It's Conan Doyle. I'll handle it, Sung. If I need you, I'll ring." He pulled the door open and stood aside.

Two men brushed by Darnell, stomping rainwater off their boots and shaking it from their coats. Doyle grasped Darnell's hand. "John. So glad you're home. You must come with us."

"You look terrible, Arthur. What's wrong?"

"This is Robert Brent, Lloyd George's secretary."

"The Prime Minister?" Darnell looked from one to the other. "What's happening?"

"His daughter, Megan, disappeared tonight," Doyle said. "A medium was conducting a séance I had arranged at Number Ten Downing. We were trying to reach his deceased daughter, Mair."

Darnell could see Doyle was really worried and that this was serious, not a prank of any kind. He wondered about the new Prime Minister, spiritualism and Doyle's hand in it. That alone could be a political problem. "Tell me how the little girl disappeared."

"I persuaded Lloyd George to hold the séance— you know my views. It's my fault. In the middle of the séance, all the lights just went out. When they were turned back on, she was gone. Vanished."

"Did you call the police?"

"David wouldn't hear of it. Said the press would tear him apart on the séance business. I told him you could help."

"The house was searched?"

"Of course, of course. But we're losing time, John. Get dressed and come back with us to Downing Street." Doyle's eyes bore into Darnell's. "David's naturally beside himself. His wife is in shock and can hardly speak."

"Give me five minutes." Darnell ran up the stairs.

*   *   *

The automobile rattled over the rain-soaked cobble-stone streets toward the Prime Minister's residence, Doyle silent at Brent's side. Darnell sat in the road-ster's backseat feeling the rain drifting in through openings in the celluloid flaps covering the windows. He stared glumly out at the streets of London, lit ee-rily by the new yellow streetlights. The musty smell of wet stones and pavement wafted into the car.

Darnell had bid Penny a hasty good-bye, telling her where he was going, while he hurriedly dressed. Now he had time to think. A missing child. Scenes from his own childhood flashed through his mind and his frown deepened. Darnell knew how helpless the Prime Min-ister and his wife must feel. Just as his own parents had when his younger brother, Jeffrey, had disap-peared, so many years ago, as a child of seven. The dark memories flooded back into his thoughts.

When the carriage pulled up in front of the man-sion, Brent jumped out in the rain, ran to the door, and pulled it open. Darnell shook his head to clear the old memories. He and Doyle strode quickly into the house.

Lloyd George stood just inside the door. "Thank God you've come." A butler took their umbrellas and coats.

After Doyle introduced Darnell to Lloyd George, the Prime Minister led the way to the living room. As they walked, he urged Darnell, "Help me give my wife some comfort, Professor. She won't speak now. Just sits there, staring into space. Maybe she'll talk to you."

Reaching the living room, Lloyd George went straight to his wife's side. "This is Professor Darnell, dear. He'll help us."

Margaret looked up at Darnell, her eyes showing a glimmer of hope. "Can you find our Megan, Profes-sor? She's fourteen, but still my baby."

Darnell said, "I'll do my best, madam."

Lloyd George gripped Darnell's arm. "One thing

first, man. Could the spirit world have taken our daughter?"

Darnell frowned as he looked at Lloyd George and Margaret with compassion. "I know my friend, Sir Arthur, holds with spiritualism. And it's true we're dealing with something mysterious. A séance. We must investigate. But I take the practical view. I think a human agency is involved."

He realized Lloyd George's wife was listening to his every word, holding her breath. When he finished, she collapsed into tears. Lloyd George returned to her side.

Doyle whispered in Darnell's ear, "Don't rule out the spirit world. There's much in nature we don't understand."

Darnell turned his head away from the others and spoke to Doyle through tight lips. "We can debate that another time, Arthur." He faced Lloyd George. "We'll examine the room where the séance was held. I need to know the details. Then I'll be able to advise you. I'll do everything in my power to help."

Sitting opposite Conan Doyle at the round table under the bright light, the table where the séance had occurred just hours earlier, Darnell continued to be astonished by the strange circumstances they faced together this night. Doyle told him every detail of the séance: how the group had gathered, put in the red bulb, held hands in the circle, experienced the lights going out, and discovered that the girl was gone when they flicked back on. But there was an increasing unreality about it all. Darnell speculated that one could even imagine a ghost stealing her away, then shook his head in disgust at even allowing the thought.

All the talk about the séance reminded Darnell of those nights ten years earlier at Cambridge, where he taught psychology and philosophy, and his debates then with Doyle, also a lecturer, on spiritualism, the growing obsession of the writer's life. Now a child was missing in the midst of something Doyle believed in intensely and had arranged—a séance. He could understand Doyle's deep concern and conflicting emotions. Something like this could break a man's spirit and belief system.

He eyed Doyle. "How can you believe in all this when your fictional characters are so pragmatic?"

Doyle scoffed. "Yes, Sherlock Holmes was fictional—that's the whole point. I know thousands write him letters at 221B Baker Street. But he had no real world or spirit world, just the setting of whatever words I put down on the page for him."

"You don't share the logical attitude you gave Holmes."

"We Scots, and the Irish, too, believe in strange things, even out-of-body experiences. It goes back to the Celts, and their magic powers. But I believe in spiritualism because I want to. I need to. My father— well, that's another story. I tried twice to reach my first wife, Louise, after she died, just to say good-bye. Felt guilt, you know, and wanted to get my own peace. But I failed. Maybe another time . . ."

"You have to make your own peace with that, Arthur. But let's concentrate on what you told me about the séance tonight. I want to reconstruct what happened after the lights went out."

"Go ahead."

"You were holding the right hand of their daughter, Megan, in your left hand? Correct?"

Doyle nodded. "Yes. A slim, dainty little hand, at that."

"And when the lights went out, what happened?" He pushed hair back from his forehead. "Her hand was still in yours?"

"Yes. The room was pitch dark. Her hand was in mine; then suddenly it wasn't, nor was Brent's, on the other side. In fact, we all dropped hands."

"All right, now concentrate on Megan." Darnell studied him. "Think . . . Did you feel anything different about her hand than you did, say, about Brent's? When you all dropped hands?"

Doyle's forehead creased with a deep frown. As if to help reenact the experience, he laid each arm out, one to the left, one to the right, closed his hands, then opened them.

"Can you recall the feeling?" Darnell prompted. "Do you remember anything unusual about Megan?"

Doyle nodded vigorously. "Yes—now I know. There *was* a difference. It seemed to me her hand was *pulled* out of mine. Then, a second later, I dropped Brent's hand."

"You say, 'her hand was pulled out of mine.' You mean, she pulled it out?" Peering over the top of his gold-rimmed reading glasses, Darnell searched Doyle's face.

Doyle frowned. "No, actually. As I think of it now, it was a more forceful feeling than her little hand could apply."

"So someone pulled her hand out of yours. Someone who took her from this room, and then away from her home."

"Someone from the spirit world? Their daughter, Mair?"

Darnell shook his head and made a sound in his throat. "Someone, Arthur, from this world. And when we find out why she was taken, we'll be able to find her. That's what I'll tell the Prime Minister and his wife."

Walking back to the living room, Darnell said, "Abduction is one of the most vicious crimes, and usually involves a helpless child. My family had that experience when I was a boy."

Doyle looked at him quizzically and was about to speak, but Darnell continued, "I'll tell you about that later. I have a feeling, Arthur, there's a very insidious element here. Something sinister, deeper, under the surface. This is not an ordinary crime."

Doyle muttered, "Spirits. It has to be."

They found Lloyd George holding his tearful wife close to him in their same seats in the living room.

Their red eyes and puffed features told the story of their worry. Lloyd George stood and faced them as they entered.

The two men, with their above-average height, towered over the Prime Minister—Darnell's frame slim but muscular at exactly six feet, Doyle's stocky, tall, and equally imposing. Inspecting Lloyd George more closely now, Darnell realized why some in the press called him a "dandy." He had a proud, strutting stance. He was dressed nattily, with his trademark bow tie, striped vest, and spats. His once-brown longish hair and brush mustache, turned now to a distinguished silver, added to the overall impression. This night, however, Darnell found Lloyd George's disheveled and haggard appearance much at odds with his normally polished look.

"Prime Minister," Darnell said. "Arthur and I have gone over everything that happened during the séance. I've reached one important conclusion."

Lloyd George and his wife looked up expectantly.

"Arthur believes the spirit world may be involved, and, of course, it did happen during a séance. But I don't hold with spirits. I suspect your daughter was kidnapped. The séance may be the key to it, a device, but not the cause. A dark room, lights going out, your daughter pulled away from Arthur, mysteriously missing when lights come on. The scene smacks of the occult. But it could be simply a vicious, planned, real-world crime."

"But who would take our daughter?" Margaret's tremulous voice echoed on the ceiling like a subdued scream.

Lloyd George said, "Are you sure it isn't the spirit world?"

"I've investigated mysterious events that smacked of paranormal manifestations, but were explainable. But I advise you to call in Scotland Yard now. I know you want privacy, but they have the resources, the people. And we need to work fast."

Lloyd George shook his head. "I made that clear—"

"But, David," his wife's voice interrupted. "We need the police. We need their help, too. Please, David. It's my baby."

"But the public . . ." Lloyd George frowned, put his arm around his wife's shoulders, and looked at Darnell. Then he sighed. "You're right, Professor. I haven't been thinking too clearly on this. I'll just warn the Yard not to release anything to the public."

Robert Brent, who had been listening to the exchange, said, "I'll call Scotland Yard, and get an Inspector here."

"Yes," Lloyd George said. "Do that at once."

Darnell said, "Doyle and I will wait here, give the Inspector the details, and discuss their plans. Then, if you want me to do my own inquiries, I'll begin at once . . ." He looked at the Prime Minister.

Lloyd George nodded. "Yes, yes, we need your assistance, Professor, and Arthur's, as well as the police. I'll have Robert draw up a letter of authorization for your investigations, to give you carte blanche. Talk to whomever you see fit."

"And I'll do anything, David." Doyle spread his arms wide. "Anything at all."

The Prime Minister said, "Thank you, Arthur." He turned to his secretary. "All right, Robert. Call the yard."

Within the hour, now approaching one A.M., the butler ushered in a short, stocky man wearing a long overcoat and a scarf bundled about his neck. He clenched an unlit pipe in his teeth and held his hat in his hand. A shock of snow-white hair topped his weathered face.

"Chief Inspector Bruce Howard," he announced, and shook hands all around. "So sorry, Prime Minister, to hear of all this. You're in good hands with the Professor, here." He nodded somberly at Darnell. "We've worked together before—the Leeds Castle case, eh, John?"

Darnell nodded. "The Prime Minister needs official

help, Bruce, all the resources of your offices." He faced Lloyd George. "If you please, Prime Minister, Arthur and I will tell the Chief Inspector what we know, and come back to make our plans."

Lloyd George said, "Do it. I'll have coffee made."

Again, Doyle and Darnell walked down to the sé-ance room, this time with the Inspector. They showed him the scene and told him everything that had transpired.

"This is too much for me," Chief Inspector Howard said. "Séances. Spirits. Give me an old-fashioned bur-glary or bludgeoning. I can deal with that kind of thing."

Darnell agreed. "Maybe we can divide up what we do, move faster, and keep each other informed."

"Good. You take the mystics. I'll take the rest."

Over the next half hour, Howard quickly inter-viewed the household staff, who shed no light on the events. He said he'd have other officers continue that the next day. Afterward, he talked gently with Lloyd George and Margaret as Darnell and Doyle observed, beginning with the single question he felt was signifi-cant. "Is there anything you can tell me that would shed light on this?"

Lloyd George shook his head. "I can't think . . . No, nothing."

"The rest of your family? Where are they?"

Margaret answered in tremulous voice. "Our two sons, Gwilym and Richard, and our daughter Olwen Catherine, are all away at college. Our only child still with us all the time is our dear Megan . . ." She choked up and her eyes filled with tears.

"All right, we'll save any other questions for tomor-row." He rose and faced Lloyd George. "We'll be back first thing tomorrow with our best people, Prime Minister."

Lloyd George asked, "Where will you start, Pro-fessor?"

"I'll begin with our mystery woman, the medium Ilena Ispenska. If spiritualism is involved in this crime, even indirectly, she could be the key to solving it."

Chapter 3

Friday morning, December 15, 1916

Not wanting to wake his wife, John Darnell opened the bedroom door softly, but Penny opened her eyes. "John? What time is it?" She turned over in bed toward him, yawning.

"Three a.m. Sorry. I'll tell you about it in the morning." In minutes, he was in bed and asleep, dreaming of séances.

At breakfast, Sung served toast, bacon, eggs, cereal, and juice. "Put on some more coffee, Sung," Darnell said. "This is a two-pot morning."

Darnell touched his lips to Penny's as he refilled her cup and his own. Her perfume mingled with the fragrance of the breakfast, and all his senses were alive. "Wish I didn't have to leave this morning," he said.

"I know, duty calls." Penny smiled. She caressed the back of his neck. "That poor girl. Fourteen, just the age of Sung's son. You think the medium is involved in the disappearance?"

"If you're asking 'Could spirits have taken someone who disappears during a séance?' Arthur thinks so. Of course, I say no. The medium's involvement? That remains to be seen."

"And Scotland Yard?"

"They deal with this world, and I think one is

enough for them. So we compromised. They'll talk with the Prime Minister's family and aides. Conan Doyle and I will take a closer look at the medium this morning."

Penny said, "So, Conan Doyle, the great detective-story writer becomes a detective, too." She reached for the toast tray and buttered a crisp slice.

"He's done it before," Darnell said. "And Arthur knows a lot about séances. He's seen phony mediums as well as what he calls sincere ones. He's deep into studies of the spirit world."

"I'm surprised a serious writer believes in spiritualism."

Sung interrupted, bringing coffee. Darnell munched on his eggs and toast.

In a moment he said, in a serious tone, "Millions swear by spiritualism today. It's that desperate wish to talk with those who've gone beyond." He paused. "There's something I've never told you, Penny . . . My mother and father . . . well, they had a great loss. And I did, too. When I was a child."

Penny stared at him. "Tell me about it, John."

He swallowed. "It's difficult to talk about . . . my younger brother, Jeffrey. He disappeared two years before we moved to England. I was eight, and Jeff seven."

Penny leaned over and put her arm around his shoulder. She saw moisture in his eyes. "Why haven't you told me about this before, dear?"

"Even after all these years, it's still painful." He went on. "Police scoured the city and countryside, but never found Jeff. I remember my mother and father argued—she wanted desperately to have a séance, but, as a minister, Father refused. Finally, we moved from America to England. Mother told me it was the only way they could forget, and start over. None of us ever spoke of it again."

Penny held him close. "So you know how Lloyd George and his wife must feel."

"Only a little, not as a parent. I was quite young.

But I'll never forget that night Jeff didn't come home . . .
and the way my mother cried. I guess that's one reason I have to do whatever I can to help. It's so much
like my own brother's case."

Conan Doyle arrived in his own motorcar at exactly
nine o'clock, and waited at the curb in front of the
flat. Hearing the car pull up, Darnell grabbed his coat,
kissed Penny, and said a quick good-bye. He hurried
out, carrying a piece of toast.

Darnell jumped into the passenger seat of the open
car. He smiled at Doyle's dust glasses, and said,
"You're a race driver?"

"Have to see the road," Doyle said.

"You have the directions to Madame Ispenska's?"

"Yes, I've been there to interview her. It's about
twenty minutes from here. There's a few twists and
turns. We go down Kensington past the park and over
to Piccadilly."

After Doyle had pulled into traffic and settled down
into his driving, Darnell asked, "What's your opinion
of Madame Ispenska? Is she real?"

Doyle said, "Her mother, a gypsy, was a medium
before her. I've known many mediums. Some sincere,
some charlatans."

"How can you tell them apart, the phonies from
those you'd consider sincere?"

"Fakes use gimmicks and devices. One medium had
a device that put out smoke, making it look like a
ghost. Another had a contrivance allowing her to lift
the entire table with her knees. They try to simulate
ectoplasm, with steam and chemicals. And they produce hidden objects seemingly out of the thin air. The
objects are called 'apports.' Sometimes phony mediums will hide them in their bulky clothes, and then
pop them out in the dark."

"What about our case, communicating with spirits?"

"So-called 'mental mediums' find out tricks of
speech of the deceased, their favorite words, how their
voices sounded, and pieces of personal information.

If they're fakes, they mimic their talk. But it sounds quite real."

"And the ones you call sincere?"

"Some are real, and they do get through to the other side. I'm convinced of it. Once I felt a hand on my shoulder in a dark séance room, and not from a participant, all were holding hands. I swear it was no one from this world."

"A spirit? You think that?" Darnell knew he and Conan Doyle would always differ on this kind of evidence.

"I felt it was." He glanced sidelong at Darnell. "I know you're skeptical. But keep an open mind. True, Shakespeare spoke of *'The undiscovered country, from whose bourn no traveller returns.'* Yet who knows what commerce can pass between these two worlds?"

Darnell muttered, "We're in the twentieth century now." Then, "Let's get back to Madame Ispenska, Arthur. Is she one of your sincere mediums, as you call them, or a charlatan?"

"I felt she was one who had real powers. She didn't do anything bizarre. No reason to change my mind."

The car rattled along the road. "Not far now," Doyle said. "We pass Piccadilly Circus, and take the left fork off the square."

Darnell nodded. In his mind's eye he tried to visualize the woman and her domicile. Soon enough, he'd see her.

They fell into silence as the car puffed and clanked along the streets of London. They entered a cobblestone side street leading across to another boulevard, Doyle concentrating on his driving. Darnell watched the other cars as they passed and reflected that each day he saw more automobiles on the road, newer models, and fewer horses and carriages. He felt autos would soon take over the streets completely. He watched an autobus carrying twenty or more people clattering by in the other direction. His nose wrinkled with the exhaust fumes. Progress, he thought, had its price.

Doyle broke the silence. "The war news is discouraging."

"What? Oh, yes, yes . . . it's a stalemate, I'd say."

"We have the edge. But no one wins a war, when you're losing a million men a year. There are no real victories. And yet the atmosphere of war is wonderful—the camaraderie, the daring, the heroism."

"There's not much glory in a million deaths."

"Agreed." Doyle added softly, "I have two sons in the war. I'm worried they'll be part of those forgotten millions."

"Are your sons in the thick of it?"

"They're officers. That may save them. I pray it does."

They came to the square and took the left.

Darnell studied Doyle. "As a doctor, you take an unusual interest in war. It seems contrary to your calling."

Doyle shook his head. "Who better than a doctor? I've seen it all. I've sailed as a ship's surgeon to the Arctic and Africa, harpooned whales, and shot alligators. But treating men shot in battle, or for enteric fever—that's the worst experience of all."

"You speak of the Boer War, and your experiences there."

He nodded. "I wanted to fight, but was too old. So I went as a doctor. I learned more than I wanted to know about warfare in Africa. Served as war correspondent. You know about my war history and pamphlets. Something you don't know . . ." He gestured toward the heavens. "The war led me deeper into spiritualism."

"The war did?"

"Soldiers often see apparitions on the battlefield. And they watch buddies die in battle. After the Boer War, ten years ago, many mothers wanted to reach sons who'd died. Spiritualists and séances offered a means of bridging the two worlds."

He mused. "Mothers could reach sons they lost, grieve one last time, and find peace. But not much was done for the returning soldiers. Their minds were all torn up."

Darnell thought of his mother, and Jeff's disappearance, how she wanted to call in a spiritualist, how his father refused. "Do you believe mediums can reach them, those sons who died?"

"Yes, I do. I've heard a departed son ask—through the medium's voice, of course—'Are you happy?' The poor mother or wife would respond, 'Now I am.' " Doyle mused. "Unless the medium was a fraud—and some are—I believed it. One thing, the mothers felt better. Perhaps that's what is important, after all. The need to contact those sons has developed again, in this war. Mediums are busy these days."

Doyle slowed as he started down the narrow side street, and Darnell checked the numbers on the large, frame houses.

"We're coming close now, one of these houses. They all look alike," Doyle said. "Watch for 666. The devil's number."

"Here it is," Darnell said.

Doyle headed the auto into the curb and pulled up the stiff hand brake. "I wonder if she picked this house just for that devil number. She claimed not."

"She's a medium, not a witch, Arthur. I'd say she either has a bizarre sense of humor, or it's just a coincidence."

As they stepped out of the open car and dusted off their coats, Doyle removed his driving glasses and stuffed them into a pocket. He handed an envelope to Darnell. "Here's Lloyd George's authorization letter, if she questions us."

Darnell led the way up to the front door and rapped on it. "Get your cross out, Arthur." Darnell smiled. "Just in case."

Doyle stomped up the stairs behind him. "The first time I came here, I fully expected the devil to step out."

A woman's hand pulled the drape back from a long window next to the door, and Darnell found himself staring into the black eyes of a woman looking out at them. Her face was partially covered with a shawl. When the drape closed, Darnell said, "She must be the mystery woman."

After several long moments, the door creaked open, and Madame Ilena Ispenska stood in front of them. "I expect you. The child—you are here about her, yes?" She stood aside and bowed low. "Come in."

They stepped into the dark-paneled, musty entry hall. Doyle introduced Darnell and the medium to each other, and quickly asked, "How did you know we're here about the girl?"

"She was taken last night in the séance. I have the perception."

Seeing their expressions, she offered a smile, but Darnell thought it did nothing to improve her looks. She added, "The Prime Minister's man also called me."

"Brent?"

"Hugo Stanton, his aide who interviewed me." She paused. "You have not found her, or you would not be here."

"No, we haven't," Darnell said. "We have a few questions . . ."

Madame Ispenska interrupted, her hands fluttering in the air. "No, no, not now. A séance is about to begin. People are already in the room."

Darnell glanced at Doyle to see his expression, then said to her, "We can observe, stay in the background, and not disturb you." The chance to watch her was fortuitous.

Doyle nodded. "You owe this to us, Madame Ispenska. It was I who gave your name to the Prime Minister."

"I know that . . . but it is very unusual for anyone but the family to be present." The medium frowned, but at last nodded. "Yes. This once. But do not interfere. Follow me."

She led the way down a long hallway and took them into a large, windowless room with three walls covered by blood-colored drapes. She locked the door, but left the key in the lock.

"Ladies and gentlemen," she said, "these two men wish to observe. They will disturb nothing."

A silver-haired woman dressed in black spoke in answer, "I know him," and all eyes turned toward Doyle and Darnell. "It's Dr. Doyle," the elderly woman went on. "Yes, he can stay, with his friend. We need believers."

Doyle and Darnell took chairs placed against the wall.

The medium took her place at one end of the oval table, and those around the table joined hands. Madame Ispenska pressed a switch attached to the table and all lights went out except a dim red bulb over the table.

Doyle whispered to Darnell, "The diffused red light is supposed to make it more comfortable for the spirits."

"At least it makes it seem more mysterious," Darnell answered in a low voice. "Do you know the woman who spoke?"

Doyle shook his head. "I don't remember her, but she seems to recall me from the old days, maybe at Southsea. She called me Doctor. If I'd seen her recently, she'd have said 'Sir Arthur.'"

Madame Ispenska spoke to the other six persons at the table. "Do not talk or break hands, no matter what happens. Today, we wish to reach the valiant son of Mary Marchant, beloved Daniel, who died at the battle of the Somme. Be patient."

She rested her head back on the chair. It seemed to Darnell she closed her eyes, but in the darkness he could not be sure. Minutes passed. The atmosphere in the room became oppressive, and so quiet he could hear the deep breathing of the others.

Darnell guessed a half hour had expired when he heard a moan come from the medium's lips. The sound wavered up and down several times, then stopped abruptly when a voice came from her mouth, not her voice but deeper, with a rasp. *"Mother, Mother, I am here."*

Darnell heard the elderly woman at the table draw in her breath sharply and say the one word, "Oh!"

"Mother. Do not fear. It is Daniel."

"Daniel! My boy." Her voice choked.

A murmur of voices came from around the table.

Doyle whispered to Darnell, "Listen carefully."

The voice from the medium's lips said, *"Mother. Don't worry. I am all right."*

"My son."

"Are you happy?" The voice came, deep and solemn, as if from a grave.

"I'm happy to hear you speak."

"Tell Missy I love her."

"Yes, yes." The mother's voice choked again.

"I am tired. I must say good-bye."

"Don't go."

The medium shook her head, sat upright in her chair, and coughed harshly. Those around the table dropped hands, and a loud buzz of conversation started. All eyes were fixed on Madame Ispenska.

"Was he here?" She looked at the mother at the other end of the table. "Did he speak?"

The woman nodded and answered, "Yes. And he spoke of Missy, his widow. She wouldn't come with me today."

The medium switched on the bright lights. "For today, it is over. We try again next week, yes?"

The white-haired woman said, "Yes. We will."

"Bring his widow."

"I'll try to persuade her." The others pushed back their chairs and stood, three elderly women and two men of their age, in addition to the mother. They all shook the hand of the medium, who stood near the doorway now, nodding, saying good-byes.

The elderly woman spoke to Conan Doyle. "You treated me for rheumatism and sciatica in Southsea, Doctor. I'm glad you believe as I do."

"I'm sorry you lost your son in the war," Doyle

said. He patted her hand, and she stepped through the doorway. "There are a million mothers exactly like her," Doyle told Darnell.

When all had left and they heard the front door close, Madame Ispenska walked with them toward the front of the house. She stopped in the entryway.

Darnell asked, "If you enter into a trance, are you aware of the words that are said, through you, by the . . . spirit?"

She shook her head. "I hear nothing, remember nothing. In the trance, everything is blank. The departed speak through me, take over my speech."

"In their own voices?"

"I'm told sometimes it sounds like the person, sometimes not. It sounds different, when dead speak."

"And you believe that happens?"

She scoffed. "Of course. When all things are right."

"And at Ten Downing Street, what happened there that you can tell us?"

"Nothing. My trance, it was cut short. I wake up, and find all the lights out."

"And Lloyd George's daughter last night? What can you tell us about her disappearance?"

"I know nothing. I was in another level. And the mother said later the girl went to her room."

"That was more than a coincidence—a séance, a dark room, and the girl disappears."

In a tense voice, she said, "I had nothing to do with it. I do not steal little girls away."

"All right, but you claim to have extrasensory perception, don't you?" Darnell pressed. "What do your senses tell you?"

The medium's brow creased. "If I went to that room again, perhaps I could feel something. I would try. That is all I can say."

"Could Megan have been drawn into the spirit world?" Doyle asked.

"I have never seen that happen—but last night, the forces were very strong. I felt a presence. But in the trance, it was like I was not there. Dr. Doyle . . . you saw more than I did.''

Darnell glanced at Doyle, who nodded.

"Yes, of course," Darnell said, with a sigh. "The trance. Well, we'll take no more of your time just now, Madame."

She opened the door for them and bowed low, gathering her shawl about her as they stepped out onto the front porch. Doyle thanked her, and she said, "Good-bye." The door closed.

Darnell breathed deeply of the crisp wintry air. "It's good just to be outside again. It's like a dungeon in there."

Doyle grumbled, "It always is. Nature of the beast." He pulled the dust glasses from his pocket as they reached the car.

"What do you make of her now, Arthur? A fake, or real?"

"She had her audience convinced. The mother."

Darnell said, "She seems to want another séance. Might be able to feel something in the same room, she said. Of course it may just be the money."

"Another séance, another twenty pounds. Still . . ."

"Arthur . . . this may not be a paranormal case at all, just a kidnapping. A police matter. Why do we persist in this?"

Doyle scowled. "Whether it's paranormal or not isn't our problem, John. It's the Prime Minister's daughter, so we have to do everything we possibly can. I feel guilty about this—and I need your help, too. With your background, you may provide some piece of information or evaluation that will be critical."

"I'll stay on it as long as he wants me, of course. But we should hurry. We're joining forces with Inspector Howard and his people at Downing Street at noon. They've got to scour the city. There's no time to lose. Somewhere, a little girl is scared to death. She may be in danger of losing her life. And not from spirits."

Chapter 4

Friday afternoon, December 15, 1916

Bruce Howard's thick Scottish brogue greeted Darnell and Doyle as they entered Lloyd George's study. He presented a uniformed woman to them. "This is Sergeant Catherine O'Reilly. She's our first female Sergeant. But she has invaluable experience with kidnappings. I've filled her in on our discussions . . . So far, there's no news of the girl."

Darnell looked at the plain, earnest face and slight frame of the uniformed woman with some surprise as he extended his hand. A female Sergeant with curly blond hair—Scotland Yard was changing. "Very pleased to meet you, Sergeant." He glanced over her shoulder at the face of Inspector Howard behind her. The Inspector winked.

The Sergeant gave Darnell a slight smile. "I've heard of your work, Professor. I hope you and I can pool our resources."

"Exactly. We need to find Megan fast." As he said the words, Darnell's thoughts flashed back to the seven-year-old face of his lost brother, his mother's tearful face, and her words to the police, *"Please find him."* He cleared his throat. "Madame Ispenska said she remembers nothing at all that happens when she's in a trance. Dead end, there."

Seeing the Prime Minister's expression sag at his

words, Darnell felt compelled to add, "Of course, we're just starting on this." He glanced at Doyle, who stood at the window, staring morosely out at the cloudy sky. Doyle nodded, without turning his head.

"Séances are fascinating," Sergeant O'Reilly said, "but I'll leave that realm to you. I want to interrogate the staff, here and at the Prime Minister's offices, and go through files. We're looking for a motive."

"I agree with that. The important thing now," Darnell said, "is to find out why this happened. When we know why someone took Megan, we'll be able to find her."

Lloyd George expelled a deep breath. "Maggie's imagining all manner of things."

"We'll work as fast as we can," Chief Inspector Howard said. "But there's something we must consider . . . something I, well, hesitate to bring up at this time."

"Out with it, man," Lloyd George burst out.

"There could be a ransom demand. We may hear today."

Lloyd George sat ramrod straight in his chair. "Ransom! From the Prime Minister? How dare they!"

Darnell asked, "This kidnapping wasn't done on the spur of the moment, Prime Minister. There's a lot of organization behind this, and, yes, they specifically targeted you as head of the government. I'm sure of that."

"What do you mean, Professor? A plot?"

"A plot, yes, sir," Darnell said. "Targeted at you, because of your position. So we must look into your recent life to see what might trigger this—ask about your enemies, any major disputes with your associates."

When Lloyd George turned to question the Chief Inspector, Darnell focused his attention on photos he'd noticed on the walls. He studied pictures of the Prime Minister with King George V and various other world dignitaries, including a photo of a somewhat younger Lloyd George with Kaiser Wilhelm. Recent battlefields were circled in red on a large map on one wall.

Sergeant O'Reilly took a chair in front of Lloyd George's desk. "This might relate to your daughter's life, Prime Minister. Did she have anyone jealous of her? Any questionable friends?"

Lloyd George scowled. "None of that. Megan's a good girl. Just a child, at fourteen. In my case? I became Prime Minister a week ago, and a lot of people were upset by my selection. *The old order changeth*— and I'm the one ordering the changes."

"Could it be revenge, Prime Minister?" O'Reilly asked.

"I don't know." Lloyd George's frown deepened.

"Anything else controversial?" Darnell asked.

"This damned war, of course. We're two years into it, at a stalemate, and we've lost a million men, sons and husbands. Their families want someone to blame, and that has to be me."

Darnell went on, "What about the proposal for peace discussions from Germany?"

"Those damned things." Lloyd George fumed. "The pacifists want peace at any price. The Germans send out feelers, and the press publicizes them. Now President Wilson wants us to look at them, although the Yanks aren't even involved."

Conan Doyle turned from the window toward them, and his deep voice filled the room. "Don't even consider it, David. America has no stake in this war, at least not yet."

"I agree, Arthur. But our generals say the war could go on for years."

"We'll win, if you watch out for their subs."

Lloyd George stood and paced back and forth. "You're like a nagging conscience, Arthur. They've got a hundred and fifty subs, and they worry me, too. If they block our food supply, I'll have to use convoys."

Doyle persisted. "Remember my airships warning? I expect they were helpful."

Lloyd George nodded. "I know. They dropped thirty-five thousand pounds of bombs on London before the War Cabinet put machine guns on our planes.

Well, I've cut the cabinet from twenty-three to five. We'll move faster now." He stopped pacing. "But no more war talk! I want Megan back home with me and her mother. While she's missing . . . it's too much . . ." His voice choked. "How can I fight the war, comfort my poor wife . . . ?"

Sergeant O'Reilly glanced at Inspector Howard for guidance. He held a hand toward her, palm out, a signal to hold back for a moment.

Doyle spoke to Lloyd George. "I have an idea, David. Hold another séance here, tonight. The medium said she might learn more about Megan's disappearance if she were back in the same room."

"A second séance? My God." He looked at Darnell. "Professor?"

"You know my feelings. Yet . . . if nothing else, it could prove spiritualism had nothing to do with it." He paused, then added, "A seemingly paranormal mystery that began with one séance could end with another."

Lloyd George shook his head. "I don't know if my wife can go through all that again." He looked at Doyle. "Arthur? You're the spiritualist. Are you sure?"

"Not sure of anything except maybe we should try it. If it proves nothing, we can at least go on from there with a clean slate."

After a moment, Lloyd George said, "All right. Will you get Madame Ispenska here, Arthur? We'll begin at seven tonight."

Doyle said, "I'll bring her myself."

Lloyd George spoke in a stern voice. "I'm going to invite one or two trusted friends to observe. I need objective opinions now."

"I'll leave evaluation of this to you, Professor," Sergeant O'Reilly said, rising from her chair. "The Yard doesn't have a séance department. But I'll be here. To observe."

"Of course." Darnell said. He knew it was time to go now. They'd said what had to be said. Hearing of Lloyd George's heavy war burdens had given Darnell an idea of how much the man had on his mind.

"We'll be here, then, David, at seven," Doyle said. "Tell Margaret she has nothing to fear from the spirit world."

As he left, Darnell added, "One thing. If there is a plot, we may learn whether Madame Ispenska is involved in it."

Robert Brent stood outside the Prime Minister's office, hesitating. Should he carry on with his duties, work on the correspondence, or simply go home. It was still early . . .

Then he heard the voice, of someone apparently on the telephone, speaking, then silent, then speaking again, in a low tone. Visitors and officials had been in and out of Ten Downing all day, and he wondered who it was. The voice was muffled, at the other side of the office, and the office door was open only an inch or two.

Brent strained to hear the words, knowing it was not Lloyd George's voice and that normally no one should be alone in the Prime Minister's office. Then he recognized the voice. The words he could hear bothered him, but he was timid about entering and confronting the speaker. He walked on to the front door and out to the street.

He motioned for his car to be brought around. But as he stood, thinking about the words, he frowned deeply. He turned and strode purposefully back inside the house. But when he reached the office he found no one there. Should he talk with the Prime Minister about it? He'd have to think that through.

John Darnell unlocked the front door of his flat just as the hall grandfather's clock chimed twice for the half hour. Three-thirty p.m. Sung would be preparing their tea, always served promptly at four.

"Penny," he called, and headed toward the stairs.

She called from the sitting room. "I'm in here, John."

As he stepped through the doorway, Penny quickly moved across the room and into his arms. She loos-

ened his tie and collar. "I missed you." Darnell kissed
her and held her tight.

When they broke apart, he moved to the server
where a cream sherry bottle and glasses rested. He
filled two of the delicate small glasses and handed one
to Penny. They touched glasses and he took a generous swallow, as she sipped hers.

"We watched a séance this morning at Madame Ispenska's house," he said. "We met with Scotland Yard
this afternoon. And there'll be another séance tonight—seven o'clock, at Downing Street."

"You're enjoying these séances." Penny's eyes
twinkled.

Darnell scoffed. "Not bloody likely. But Doyle
does. I think he believes in them even more than he
admits." His eyes narrowed. "And that medium, Madame Ispenska. Something about her bothers me. I
suspect she's an accomplished fraud."

"A fraud? Well, aren't they all?"

"Doyle tells some humorous stories about them—
fake ectoplasm, devices hidden under their garments,
horns blown by confederates, imitations of the voices
of deceased loved ones. Frauds, all. I would believe,
from that. But then Doyle tells of hands touching his
shoulder during a séance."

Penny shivered. "Brrr." She pulled him down next
to her on a plush sofa. "All right, sit," she said. "And
don't move until after teatime."

He smiled, and sat next to her. He went on, "Doyle
would argue many if not most mediums are legitimate."

"Meaning what? They can really talk with the dead?
Really, John."

"I didn't say that—he did. The dead have their
world, and we have ours, regardless of Doyle's
beliefs."

"Two great minds, two opposite belief systems."

"You know my feelings on all of this. It's my profes-
sion to prove none of it is true."

"That should be easy. It's all hogwash." Penny

laughed at the look on his face. "That's one of our Texas sayings."

They finished their sherry just as Sung appeared, rapping on the open door.

"Come in," Penny called.

Sung brought a silver tray laden with teapot, cups, sugars, thick creams, and slices of cake. He placed it on a table in front of the couch. "Tea, Mr. and Mrs.," he said, eyes smiling.

"You love to say Mr. and Mrs., don't you?" Penny smiled. "Even after four years."

"Yes, Mrs. Penny. It reminds me of all good things that happen, since you came here. Having my son with me, growing up in England now."

"How's your son doing in school lately?" Penny watched as Sung poured tea into their cups.

"Very fine," Sung said with a broad smile. "Ho San loves the English schools. Has learned so fast." He bowed slightly from the waist, glancing at Darnell, who had been urging him to abandon his quaint bowing custom.

Darnell winked at Sung and said, "You can bow out, too." As Sung left, Darnell said, "Teatime. Let's try Sung's special Chinese orange cake."

Later, Sung cleared the tea things away, left the room, and closed the door.

Penny leaned her head against Darnell's shoulder and sighed. "You've been neglecting me, John. You were out late last night, gone all day today in séances . . ."

"But you've been keeping busy with your charity work?"

She frowned. "Yes. It's so depressing, though. Talking with those poor soldiers, with all manner of wounds. Those recovery homes . . . some of the men have to stay there for months."

"You're doing valuable work."

"I hope so. Sometimes when I'm in the back rooms, just rolling bandages . . . I don't know, I wonder. But when I talk with them, hear their stories, and see them smile a bit—it does seem I'm doing something worthwhile."

"You need to get out and do something lighter sometimes."

Penny sighed. "I will. But let's talk about your séance again. Tell me what she looks like."

"Who—the Sergeant? Oh, ah, rather plain . . ." Darnell raised his eyebrows and searched for words.

Penny grabbed his arm. "A female Sergeant? You're holding back on me, John Darnell. I meant Madame Ispenska, the medium." She teased. "You're meeting with two *femmes fatales*?"

Darnell laughed. "Don't worry. Madame Ispenska won't mesmerize me. As to Sergeant O'Reilly, the Chief Inspector says she'll be valuable after finding that kidnapped boy last year. But she's not at all, shall we say, arresting." He smiled.

"Yes, yes, I'll bet. You professors know all the right words, all the funny words, how to deflect a question. But two women are still two women."

"How can a violet-eyed woman like you have such green eyes?" Darnell pulled her closer to him, feeling the smooth texture of the silk dress that clung to her body. "You're the arresting one, the mesmerizing one, for me." He pressed his lips to hers.

Penny breathed, "It's only four-thirty, John. We have two hours before you go back to Downing Street." She pushed the hair back from his forehead.

Darnell laughed. They rose and walked toward the staircase, arm in arm.

As Sung walked by the staircase toward the kitchen, he saw them walking up to the second floor. He caught a few words, and smiled at Penny's musical laughter and Darnell's husky voice.

The grandfather's clock struck twice, as Ho San stepped into the entryway at four-thirty p.m. Sung motioned to him.

Sung said, "Come, son, we go to kitchen for a while. Study your homework." He smiled. "Mr. and Mrs. raising spirits."

Chapter 5

Friday evening, December 15, 1916

Robert Brent felt at loose ends. He spent two hours in the Downing Street kitchen with the cook, drinking coffee, reading over some of his papers, stalling. He wanted to face the situation he had encountered in the Prime Minister's office, the phone call. Yet another part of him wished he could forget it. In wartime, he never knew, even as confidential secretary, whether he should be hearing certain private conversations in that awesome combination home and war office—secrets he was not authorized to hear. But that phone call was different.

Brent glanced at his watch. His next duty was to pick up Professor Darnell at his home at six-thirty. An hour to go. He decided to stop by the Prime Minister's office. If he found the Prime Minister there, he could make his decision then about what to do, and then go on to Darnell's place. With that resolution, he rose and gathered his papers.

As he entered the Prime Minister's office, he had a sense of something out of place. Then he saw it on the side table. An open briefcase. He walked to it, glanced at the initials engraved on it, and peered inside. Something odd struck him. A deck of playing cards was lying partially hidden by papers at the bottom in the case. Out of curiosity, he took the deck out and tapped a few cards into his palm. He raised his eyebrows when he saw that they were marked on their faces in a strange manner. The symbols meant nothing to him, and if there was a message in them, he could not fathom it. Hearing footsteps coming in the hall, he thrust the deck into his pocket and left the room by another door, not knowing someone watched him leave.

In minutes he had taken a circular route back to the front entrance. He went outside, breathless, and with a strange anxiety. His car, which he had ordered up two hours ago, still sat at the curb. He jumped into it and quickly drove off. He had an hour to kill, but he'd park somewhere and take a closer look at the deck of cards.

Suddenly, he felt very silly about it all, and laughed out loud. In the midst of it, he thought of the missing girl Megan, whom he'd seen so often about the home, giggling, laughing, humming little tunes, and his own laugh choked in his throat.

In the hour that he had for himself, Brent drove about slowly in the general direction of the Darnell home, then parked the car. As he sat there, watching cabs clatter by, he thought of his father, a hansom cab driver for over twenty years who saved all of his tips to put his son, Robert, through college. "Old Bobbie," as other cabbies had called his father, lived to see his son graduate from college, but not long enough to graduate himself from horse-drawn cabs to motorcars. Yet whenever Robert saw a cab, he thought of his father.

Now he took the cards out and riffled them. Yes, they were all marked in strange symbols just above the numbers. Some of them recurred. In fact, as he studied them, he saw a definite pattern of repetition. But what they meant was a mystery. The two things together though—the phone call and the cards—told him he must see the Prime Minister and pass on what he knew as soon as the séance was completed. He could imagine how Lloyd George might easily dismiss it with a smile or a wave of the hand. God knows, the Prime Minister had other more weighty things to consider. Still . . .

The hall clock chimed the half hour past six as Darnell crossed the entryway and stepped out through the door Sung held open for him. "Thanks, Sung," he said. "Don't wait up."

He took the steps down to the curb, where the secretary Robert Brent waited in a motorcar to take him to Downing Street, the government way of being sure he was on time. Twenty minutes later the two walked into the foyer of Ten Downing Street.

"This way," Brent said, leading Darnell down the hall to the same room where the first séance had been held. He closed the door as they entered.

Darnell observed the occupants of the chairs already assembled around the table. Madame Ispenska sat next to Lloyd George, then his wife Margaret and the Prime Minister's aide, Stanton. An empty chair, then an older man who looked vaguely familiar to Darnell, next to a second older man whom Darnell recognized as Bonar Law, a senior member of Lloyd George's cabinet. Sergeant O'Reilly. Another empty chair. And Doyle, next to Madame Ispenska. The two older men, the newcomers, were apparently the observers Lloyd George had mentioned.

Darnell greeted them and shook hands with the Prime Minister. Lloyd George walked him around to the two men seated at the table. "This is Bonar Law, my old friend, and Charles Adler. They're members of my War Cabinet." They stood and he shook hands with them. Brent took his seat next to Stanton, and Darnell took the seat between O'Reilly and Doyle. A circle of ten was complete.

Doyle said, "This will tell us much, John."

Across the table the War Cabinet members talked. "I'm concerned about Lloyd George," Law said. "This is a bit macabre, isn't it?"

Adler said, "Yes, but sometimes one sees truth in

it. When my sister's son died in the war, we held one. It was incredible. He was there, that boy, in that room, I know it."

Lloyd George nodded at Doyle, then Madame Ispenska. "All right, we're all here now. Let's get on with it."

"Turn the lights off." The medium gestured toward the bright lamps and Brent clicked them off. The room was plunged into the familiar, eerie red semidarkness of the dim red bulb overhead. All stretched clasped hands with their neighbors, as before.

While they waited for the others to settle, Doyle asked Darnell, "You were going to tell me something, John, last night. Something about an abduction in your family."

Darnell nodded and spoke in a low voice. "This comes close to home for me. My younger brother, Jeffrey, disappeared when we were both children." He went on, giving details of the event, such as he had relayed to Penny. The words still hurt, and he did not want to dwell on them.

Now the room hushed, and all strained to look at the medium's face. Madame Ispenska said, "Be ready now. I need complete silence. Say nothing."

The medium rested her head back, eyes closed, and a veil of silence fell over the room. Darnell could not see well in the dim light. He focused his attention on the medium, only glancing at the others. Soon, he heard her give out a soft, slight moan in a quavering voice. He waited.

The voice slowly grew in intensity. The sound stopped, and the medium now spoke in a high-pitched female voice.

Darnell was astonished to hear that the sound was totally unlike the medium's own voice. The tone suggested the still-girlish speech of a young woman.

"Mother . . . Mother . . . ," the voice came.

Margaret gasped with a sharp intake of breath. "It's Mair!"

"Don't anyone move," Doyle said in a hoarse whisper.

"Father . . . ," the voice continued.

Lloyd George groaned.

"Father . . . you must find Megan, protect her . . . bombs . . . destruction from the skies, fire, smoke, shining lights . . . death . . ."

Darnell hung on every word, searching for a trace of the medium's own voice, not knowing Mair's voice. He was amazed at what he heard, but thought whatever it was, it couldn't be true.

"Mair," Lloyd George cried out. "Where are you?"

At that instant the red light above them went out, plunging the room into complete darkness. A chorus of cries and groans came from around the table, and Lloyd George's wife shrieked.

Lloyd George's voice rose sharply above the others. "It's the damned electricity, again. Robert, can you see to it? Everyone else sit tight. Robert . . . ?"

As if in reply, the hall door banged open, against the wall. No light came from the equally black hall outside the open door.

Madame Ispenska seemed to come to her senses. "What happened? The darkness—it is another light problem?" She pulled her hand away from Darnell's.

Lloyd George grumbled. "My secretary has gone to check it."

After several minutes, during which conversation buzzed, Darnell said, "Prime Minister, perhaps one of us should assist Mr. Brent."

"You'd never find the way to the basement . . . Stanton?"

"Yes, sir."

"Would you go see if you can help Brent with the lights?"

"Of course."

Darnell heard the scraping of a chair on the wooden floor, footsteps across the floor, and the sound of the hall door hitting the wall of the room again.

Doyle said, "I don't like this at all."

Darnell asked, "Is everyone all right? Lloyd George? Margaret? Madame Ispenska?"

Their voices came eerily from the gloom.

"Yes . . . ," from Margaret.

"Hell, no!" said Lloyd George.

"Fine," from Sergeant O'Reilly.

"I am worried," from Madame Ispenska, "and my head, it explodes."

"Blasted nuisance," Doyle said.

Without warning, the red light clicked on overhead. As their eyes adjusted, their gazes all fastened on a single sight across the table. Robert Brent was slumped over, head on one arm, with the handle of a stiletto protruding from his back. Blood dripped down onto his chair.

Lloyd George shouted, "He's been stabbed!"

Margaret screamed, "Robert!" She clutched her throat with one hand and gripped the edge of the table with the other.

The medium made a retching sound, and turned her head. "I cannot stand the blood."

O'Reilly, Darnell and Doyle jumped to their feet and circled the table to Brent's side.

Doyle reached Brent first, bent over, and placed two fingers on the man's neck. He examined the face, and pulled back a closed eyelid.

Doyle shook his head and looked across the table into Lloyd George's worried eyes. "Robert's dead, David. The knife apparently penetrated his heart, and he died instantly."

"It must have happened just after the light went out," Darnell said. "We had all dropped hands, and there were exclamations, groans around the table . . ."

"Yes, and one of those was from Robert," Doyle said. "He was stabbed from behind, with someone's other hand over his mouth, to stifle any outcry." He bent down and looked at the secretary's face and neck. "Yes. Red marks there."

"We have to secure the house, and search it," O'Reilly said. "I'll call the Yard for backup."

"It's fortunate you were here, Sergeant," Darnell said.

She responded by heading for the hallway. "I'll call the Chief Inspector and get a team out," she called over her shoulder, at the doorway. "No one must leave the house."

"My God . . ." Stanton stopped inside the doorway, staring at the scene, as he returned. "I wondered about Robert . . . There was no sign of him in the cellar."

Bonar Law and Charles Adler stood at Lloyd George's side. "If there's anything we can do . . . ," Law said.

"Tell no one about this. Right now, we need secrecy."

The two men nodded.

"Take me to our bedroom, David," Lloyd George's wife said, in tears. "I have to lie down. Poor Robert. David, I never want to enter this room again."

Darnell stood at the doorway, as Lloyd George took his wife into the hallway, holding her arm. He said, "I'll begin searching the main floor, Prime Minister, then work my way around."

Lloyd George shook his head. "It's my fault, Professor. If I hadn't allowed this blasted séance, Robert would still be alive."

Darnell shook his head. "No. You're not to blame, Prime Minister." He glanced at Doyle, who stood nearby with a downcast expression. "This doesn't involve spirits or ghosts anymore, if it ever did. It's cold-blooded murder."

Chapter 6

The investigation into Brent's murder kept everyone at Downing Street into the late hours. Chief Inspector Howard brought officers out to go over the crime scene. He, O'Reilly, and Darnell questioned those at the séance and the residence staff.

They interviewed Lloyd George and his wife about Robert Brent in the sitting room off their bedroom. Neither could offer any motive for the killing.

Margaret cried much of the time, and was now overcome with renewed worries over her daughter, after Brent's murder. Her voice choked as she searched Lloyd George's eyes. "If they killed your Robert, such a nice boy, harmless and sweet, they could kill our Megan, too."

The officers brought from Scotland Yard searched the premises and inspected the grounds in the rear of the building, but found nothing to aid in solving the crime.

Doyle said to Darnell, "I've never seen anything like this in a séance. No one ever disappeared, no one was ever hurt."

Darnell commented dryly, "I wouldn't expect you'd find dead bodies trying to reach spirits."

Doyle shook his head. "You'll never understand."

Darnell turned to Stanton, who had sat on one side

of Brent during the séance. "Were you aware of any sign of Brent being stabbed, any noise or movement?"

Stanton shook his head. "All I heard was what you did. The groaning when the lights went out. There was a lot of confused noise. Then the Prime Minister asked him to look into the lights. I thought Brent went to the cellar. When the Prime Minister wanted something, Brent would jump. But then when I found my way down there, Brent wasn't in the cellar at all."

Madame Ispenska insisted, once again, "I hear nothing when I am in the trance. I know nothing of this murder."

The butler and cook and maids had stayed in their own quarters when the lights failed. "We were afraid to leave," one maid said. "I locked our door."

"A dead end," Sergeant O'Reilly said to Howard.

"I'll see this body into the morgue. Stay on as long as you need. Work with Darnell."

Lloyd George accompanied Law and Adler to the door, conversing with them, and the two cabinet members left.

Madame Ispenska and Stanton waited for instructions in the living room, while Lloyd George and his wife stayed in their bedroom.

Doyle and Darnell met with Sergeant O'Reilly in the séance room to review the events. Darnell inserted a bright light in the overhead fixture. "That's better," he said. "Devilish red bulb."

Darnell frowned. "We have four questions now instead of two—who took the girl, who killed Brent, and, in each case, why?"

O'Reilly nodded. "And who turned off the electricity? It's no coincidence it failed twice."

"There had to be two or three confederates," Darnell said. "At least one person familiar with the inside of the house, another positioned on the outside with a vehicle for escape. One turns off the electrical connections at a predetermined time. Someone enters the séance room—kills Brent. Last night, he spirits away Megan—"

At the word "spirits" Doyle looked up at Darnell. "The medium . . . ?"

"It wasn't really her idea to have either séance," O'Reilly said. "She came on request."

"True. I offered the idea—both nights," Doyle said. "And it was a hellish one." Doyle's eyes were dark-rimmed.

"Don't be too hard on yourself, Arthur," Darnell said. He rested a hand on his friend's shoulder for a moment. Then he stepped over to the hall doorway and peered at the knob and lock. "Let's think about this room, where both crimes occurred. This door wasn't locked," he said. "No key in it."

"What?" Doyle looked up at him.

"Remember at Madame Ispenska's place, Arthur, how she locked the door to the séance room, inside, apparently for privacy?"

"She left the key in the door."

"Right, but she did lock it. Here, she didn't do that."

Doyle pulled at his mustache. "Well, it's not her house—maybe she wouldn't feel comfortable doing that."

Darnell nodded. "Or it could be . . . Remember, Sergeant, when Lloyd George asked Brent to see about the lights, the door bumped against the wall? We thought it was Brent going to the cellar."

O'Reilly nodded. "That's what I thought."

"I, too." Doyle watched Darnell walk from the doorway over to the chair Brent had occupied.

Darnell said, "For anyone to cross the room and reach Brent, kill him and quickly exit in the dark, the door would have to be unlocked. There'd be no time for fumbling with keys. And if a key had been in the lock inside it couldn't be opened."

O'Reilly shook her head, which tossed her bobbed hair from side to side. "There's no evidence the medium did anything unusual. If it had been locked, Brent may have had the key. He worked here." She paused, thoughtfully. "I'll be checking the contents of his pockets at Scotland Yard in the morning."

"So it was just a fortunate coincidence the door was unlocked?" Doyle scratched his head.

Darnell looked from Doyle to O'Reilly. "Coincidence? There are no coincidences here. Both of these crimes were planned out in detail by somebody, step by step. Fortunate? Certainly not for Robert Brent."

Sergeant O'Reilly and Darnell made a further inspection of the main floor of the house, checking doors and windows for evidence of break-in. Doyle remained with Lloyd George and his wife to offer comfort.

"Let's check the cellar," Darnell suggested. He led the way to the cellar stairwell door, near the kitchen. He clicked on a switch beside the door, turning on a light over the stairwell and another hanging farther along into the basement.

"Watch your step," he cautioned, and led the way down the narrow stairs. The dank smell of dust and cool bricks greeted them. Darnell also noticed another faint odor, something medicinal.

Against the far wall, near the second overhead light, they found the electrical current box and fuses. Darnell pulled open the box door and they peered inside. "Easy to pop out a fuse or two," Darnell said.

"And then put them back in again," O'Reilly said.

"That window, and a bench, there." Darnell walked over to the window. "This looks interesting."

O'Reilly followed. She examined the window latch. "Loose. Easily pushed open. And this bench is just too convenient."

Darnell leaned against the cool brick wall. "Let's hypothesize, Sergeant. Someone with full knowledge and access to the house comes down here. He unlatches the window and puts this bench in front of it. The confederate arrives at a predetermined time, climbs in, and, again, at a specific time, removes the fuses, throwing the house into darkness."

O'Reilly nodded. "Meanwhile, upstairs, last night the kidnapper grabs the child and takes her down through the cellar and out to the street, where a partner waits in a car. And tonight someone stabs Brent and flees out in the darkness, maybe through the front door to the same car."

Darnell nodded. "More likely, with this escape route, that person comes down here again, hitches out of this window, and runs across the back garden to a waiting car on the back street." He collected his thoughts. "If that was the plan last night, he could have handed Megan out this window to his confederate. Either way, one of them had to have some knowledge of the layout in this house."

"A former employee of Lloyd George? Someone with a grudge?"

"We have to investigate that. But there's something deeper going on."

"One thing bothers me, John. Wouldn't they have trouble controlling a struggling girl of fourteen?"

"There are several possibilities. They could have gagged her. She would have been scared to death, and might not have resisted. Or maybe they chloroformed her. Even hit her or choked her into unconsciousness."

She shuddered. "Poor thing. Those cowards."

"We'll find them."

"When we do, I'll sweat confessions out of them at the Yard," O'Reilly said.

Darnell's lips twisted into a wry smile at her words, as he followed Sergeant O'Reilly back up the stairs. He could see some toughness in her, but couldn't imagine her sweating a confession out of anyone.

They entered the living room and found Madame Ispenska and Stanton waiting.

"May I leave now?" Madame Ispenska looked from one to the other. "I am exhausted." She twisted her fingers together.

The Sergeant said, "Yes, but we'll want to talk with you tomorrow. Stay in town."

Madame Ispenska inclined her head, and walked toward the door. She turned. "I will need the ride home. I ask garage man."

Neither spoke in answer, and she proceeded down the hall toward the front door.

Darnell frowned as the medium walked away, then whispered to O'Reilly, "I just don't trust that woman . . ."

O'Reilly finished it. ". . . but you can't put your finger on exactly why."

They turned back to Stanton, who sat waiting at the far end of the room. As Darnell and O'Reilly approached, he stood and asked, "Can I be of any assistance?"

Darnell waved a hand at the chairs, and the three sat down. "Perhaps. As the Prime Minister's aide, and working with him previously on the War Cabinet, you've seen employees come and go, you do interviewing and you recommend in favor of them or against?"

"Yes. He relies on me for the junior personnel."

"Would any who worked for him in his War Cabinet post have left his employ in the past few months with a grudge against the Prime Minister? Were any discharged for bad conduct, stealing, anything like that?"

"No. When people come to work for Lloyd George, they don't leave unless there are family reasons. They're very loyal. And they're examined carefully before hiring."

Sergeant O'Reilly asked, "So you could name no one who might have sought revenge by Megan's kidnapping and Brent's murder?"

"Not at all."

O'Reilly said, "Then you may leave, Mr. Stanton. Of course, we may want to speak with you further."

"Of course." He rose and left the room.

O'Reilly looked at Darnell. "Another busy day tomorrow."

"Right. Let's call it a night. Then I'll meet you here again in the morning. Nine?"

"All right."

· Darnell glanced at the standing clock in the corner. One a.m., for the second night. The lateness of the hour gave him a sharp twinge of conscience as he thought of Penny alone at home again.

Chapter 7

Friday midnight, December 15, 1916

Megan huddled in the corner of the windowless room and stared at the angled, beamed ceilings, which reminded her of the attic in her home. The events of the past terrifying hours repeated again and again in her mind as she lay prisoner in the cold room. She tried to understand why she had been taken from her home. She coughed as she remembered the foul-smelling cloth they held over her mouth.

Someone had grabbed her in the dark during the séance, as soon as the lights went out. She couldn't scream with the man's rough hand over her mouth, and in moments he pressed the cloth smelling of medicine over her nose and mouth. It made her feel sleepy and she was close to fainting. She felt him tie a gag over her mouth and nose to keep her from crying out, and some sort of knit cap over her head and eyes. She could hardly breathe, felt sick and thought she'd die from lack of air.

He carried her down long steps and she realized later he had taken her into the dank, cold cellar. She felt herself pushed up and out of a window into the thick hands of another man. Two men outside carried her across the garden to a car. She felt dizzy and weak, and couldn't resist. She tried to cry out, but only a muffled sound escaped her lips.

A man slapped her hard on the cheek and growled, "Quiet."

One tied her arms behind her with rope in the back-seat of a car, while the other drove. She felt like her world was turning around. Terror paralyzed her body, and her mind swirled with fearsome thoughts as she sank into unconsciousness.

The car slowed and stopped after some time, and she came to her senses. She heard the engine cut off, but couldn't tell how long they had driven. Two men pulled her along into another house. A door slammed behind them. She stumbled and cried in a muffled voice into the gag as they took her up several flights of stairs. They dropped her onto a bed, took the rope off her hands, left her there, trembling and sobbing, and walked away.

When she heard the door of the room slam and lock from the outside, she ripped off the gag and cap but found the room was completely dark. She was afraid to scream. All she could think of was *Why are they doing this to me? Will they hurt me?*

Now she lay in the bed, holding her knees curled up to her chin. Tears ran down her face. She didn't bother to brush them away.

A few minutes later, one man came back. In the light streaming in from the hallway, Megan watched him put a single, bare light bulb in a ceiling fixture. Through the space of the crook of her arm, which she used to conceal her face, she looked at his bony, angular body and saw that he had a hawklike, unsympathetic face. She closed her eyes in fear at the sight. The door slammed. As she heard the key turn in the lock, she began crying again.

Some minutes after he left, Megan was able to stop sobbing. She tried the door, and found it was locked. She stumbled over to the small water closet in an alcove of the room, washed her face, and looked at it in the mirror. She gingerly touched her cheek, and winced from the pain. She put cold water on it.

She heard footsteps come up the wooden stairs, and

the rattle of the key in the lock. She sat in the one chair in the room and stared straight ahead. The man brought a plate of food and a glass of water and set it on a table. Megan avoided looking at his face. She feared what he might do to her. After he left her, she nibbled on the simple food, but had no appetite.

The next time he came, hours later, again with food, she did look at him, and asked, "What are you going to do with me?"

He leered at her, but gave no reply, and she again had the feeling he might do something to her. But he did not touch her, and in a minute or so he left.

After she ate the second time, she thought of turning off the glaring light, but the bulb was too high to reach.

Her thoughts tormented her. *Will someone come for me? Why did they do this to me?* Her only comfort was a heavy sweater her mother had knitted for her. She buried her face in the familiar material when she cried, and wiped her tears on its collar. She prayed, "Bring me home, dear God, to Momma and Poppa. Bring me home."

After a while, she fell asleep, with the bright light shining down on her little form.

In the lower levels of the old house where Megan was held captive, three men sat at the kitchen table. Two smoked cigarettes, and the acrid smell of the smoke blended with other odors hanging in the air, of fried banger sausages and eggs. One poured steaming coffee into a cup, while the other two drank straight scotch whiskey from large water tumblers.

One of the men, whom the others called Slade, periodically added whiskey to his tumbler from the near-empty bottle on the table. He thumbed at the bottle, saying, "We need more of that."

Karl, hook-nosed and swarthy, wearing seaman's dungarees and jacket, nodded. "It's rotgut, but better than nothing."

Slade grinned, showing gaps for two missing teeth. "You're whispering, but who can hear?"

The windows of the deserted house were boarded,

and, even at midday, only thin shafts of light could be seen through the small cracks in the boards. The house's isolated, secluded location was down a long roadway, set back from the street.

Karl ignored Slade's comment. "Four more days," he said. He punctuated his remark with a swallow of whiskey. "I can't last that long. This place is driving me balmy."

"You complain," Slade sneered, "but I'm the one who goes up to that room." He gestured upward with his thumb. "That girl fixes those blue, sad-dog eyes on me every bloody second when I take her the food. She pretends not to look at me, but I know she's watching me." He reached for the whiskey bottle. "I'm not a bloody pervert."

Karl sneered. "Hah! She knows what's in your bloody mind better'n you do."

"Not half. As if I'd touch her . . ." Slade scowled, but looked away. He rubbed his unshaven chin.

"You'd touch her, all right, Slade. You're the type."

The third man glared at Slade. His guttural voice sliced through the room like the knife he always carried. "Keep your hands off the girl. Both of you. Touch her, and it'll be the last sex you ever have."

Baldrik folded his thick, hairy bare arms over his massive chest and stared at them, as if daring the others to respond.

Pouring whiskey into his tumbler, Slade avoided Baldrik's eyes, afraid to reveal the chill that sliced up his back at the other's words. He recalled grim rumors that fed Baldrik's ruthless reputation as a cold-blooded killer and mutilator—how, when he worked in hospital morgues, he'd carve up the corpses ready for disposal. Slade regretted his involvement with Baldrik. What good is five hundred pounds, he thought, if you're dead, or if your hand or other body parts are chopped off with a cleaver?

Slade resolved, if worse came to worst, if he felt his life was in danger, he wouldn't hesitate to slit Baldrik's throat as the man slept. He knew taking this job was

the biggest mistake he'd ever made in his twenty-three
years. Karl had talked him into the job, but now needled
him at every turn. Well, he'd pay Karl back for that.

He tossed half of the whiskey from a water glass
into his mouth and enjoyed the musty burning flavor
as it seeped down his throat. Tonight, he decided,
would be a good time to get good and blotto.

But despite Baldrik's warning, the girl's eyes burned
in Slade's mind. Maybe Karl was right. He licked his
lips. One of these times, he just might give her something to remember.

Two a.m., and Lloyd George stared into the fireplace. A roaring fire served as a mesmerizer to calm
his nerves, and he would often doze in his big chair.
But tonight his eyes wouldn't close. It was all crashing
in on him—decisions as War Minister putting thousands of lives at risk, now with even heavier burdens
as Prime Minister. But his daughter's life overshad-
owed it all. He took a large swallow from his whiskey glass.

He wondered, *Could I have averted the war?* He'd
talked with Kaiser Wilhelm's advisors at the Windsor
Castle reception in 1907. *Did I pound the table hard
enough? On the trip to Germany in 1908, could I have
built better relations with the Kaiser and his emissaries,
or was it all a lost cause?* Had England simply been
doomed, foreordained to join the war to honor that
old treaty with Belgium after Germany attacked that
small country?

Tormented, he asked himself, *Could I have coun-
seled King George V when he tried in 1914 at Bucking-
ham Palace to mediate European issues? No,* he
thought. *I did my best. It just failed.* He sighed, realizing at that moment that after Archduke Ferdinand
and his wife were assassinated in June 1914, nothing
could have changed the war's history. It was like domi-
noes, with all the countries declaring war, one after
another, within a period of only weeks.

Two years and millions of dead soldiers later, Lloyd

George knew that trench lines were dug in, and each inconclusive battle slaughtered thousands. The war was stalemated, and he was frustrated he could do nothing about it. Only Russia or America, with President Wilson reelected now in the United States, could break the stalemate.

His deepest thoughts, however, pushing all others aside, were of Megan. He knew that the murder of Brent increased her danger. They were clearly dealing with hard, cold men. Was she even still alive? Sometimes, too, he heard again in his mind the voice of Mair, saying words she seemed to speak to him at the séance.

Lloyd George shuddered and gulped the rest of his second whiskey and soda. He rang for the butler. When he arrived, he said, "Another stiff one, Phillips. It'll be a long night."

Phillips extended a silver tray to the Prime Minister with a single envelope lying on it. "I was about to bring this in to you, sir, when you rang. It came by hand messenger."

Lloyd George scowled and picked up the envelope. He nodded, and the butler bowed and left the room.

Another War Cabinet report, another crisis, he thought. They had been coming in at all hours of the day and night as battle results were known. But as he looked at the envelope, he could see it was of high linen quality with a foreign watermark.

He tore it open and read the wording printed in bold capitals on the small sheet of paper: "ACCEPT THE GERMAN PEACE PROPOSALS IF YOU WANT TO SEE YOUR DAUGHTER ALIVE AGAIN."

Lloyd George gasped and bolted to his feet. Conflicting emotions swept through his body. The House of Commons was reassembling on December 19, just three more days, and he had to deal with the peace proposals. He dreaded telling Maggie, and decided to wait until morning. But Scotland Yard and Darnell and Doyle must be reached at once. He lifted the telephone receiver, and waited impatiently for the operator to come on the line.

Chapter 8

The sound of a bell ringing seeped into Darnell's consciousness, and he realized he had been lying half-awake for some moments. He heard Sung's voice speaking downstairs. The telephone. He glanced at a clock. Past two A.M. He slipped out of bed, trying not to wake Penny, who had slept through his late arrival just a half hour earlier. Her eyes were still closed and her breathing deep.

Grabbing his robe and slippers, he strode across the room and headed down the stairs. Sung met him halfway up. "The Prime Minister," he said. "Sounds worried."

Darnell hurried by Sung, saying, "All right." Downstairs, on the phone, he said, "Darnell here, Prime Minister," and Lloyd George read him the note he had received.

"So they've shown their hand," Darnell said. He thought for a moment. "There's not much we can do until morning, Prime Minister. But Sergeant O'Reilly and I will be there at nine a.m. We'll do everything possible to get to the bottom of it."

Back in bed, Darnell stared at the ceiling for long minutes before his eyes closed again.

At seven a.m. on Saturday, Sergeant Catherine O'Reilly tossed her purse and coat on a chair by her desk in the large bay of the Yard office. Although it was staffed twenty-four hours a day, only a few officers were on duty at the Yard at that hour. The night force required few men, and the day crew hadn't arrived. Without the privacy of an office reserved for detectives and inspectors, during the day she felt like the proverbial goldfish in a bowl. She liked early mornings for gathering her thoughts on her case load with more privacy and without interruption.

Her methodical approach to cases had secured her promotion to the first female Sergeant at the Yard, at thirty-one, three months earlier. She knew her success saving the kidnapped son of the stage actress Melissa Danielle the year before played a crucial role. The *London Times* had made Catherine O'Reilly a household name for weeks in 1915 during the investigation and after her successful recovery of the boy. Now she had another huge case, involving the nation's leader. More publicity, she thought.

Although elated with her promotion, and now this new assignment, Catherine had a sinking feeling her new duties and long hours would continue to ruin opportunities for any kind of social life, and any possible matrimony. She sighed, tried to push those personal conflicts out of her mind, and addressed her work.

She opened the small cardboard box labeled "Robert Brent" and peered at the contents. She cleared a place on her desk. As she took out each item, she studied it and checked it against a list in the box. A dull routine, but she knew her methodical approach yielded results.

The contents of the box seemed ordinary enough— a ring of keys, a wallet with identification, eleven pounds in notes, coins, a linen handkerchief, another silk one, a pen and a pencil. She thought of the secretary, only twenty-three, never to know the joys of life that would come with later years—love, marriage, children, things she dreamed of herself.

Even as these thoughts plagued her, she realized she had a problem of identifying too closely with victims, a weakness that could take away objectivity. She had fought emotions tugging on her heart as she searched for Melissa Danielle's eight-year-old son. She sighed, and pushed the thoughts away. The last item in Brent's box caught her interest—a deck of playing cards.

The flap of the card box was loose. Curious, she slipped the cards out and flipped through them. Inspecting them, she raised her eyebrows as she saw various astrological symbols neatly inked on the top left corner of the cards—the sun, moon, stars, signs of the zodiac. She scanned the cards, but saw no pattern. She thrust the pack of cards and other articles back into the box of effects, and set it to one side.

A few officers were arriving now, and she stepped around to the kitchen to brew a cup of tea. Chief Inspector Howard looked up from his seat at the table as she entered the small room.

"Well, Sergeant—did you get any sleep?"

She smiled. "Not much. This kind of case, with a child involved, ruins your sleep. It's like last year again."

"I know. Poor Lloyd George. His first week as Prime Minister, and his daughter is gone missing. How much can the man take?"

O'Reilly sat opposite him with her small pot of tea and cup. She'd have a few minutes to talk, to review the case before going to Downing Street.

Howard looked around. No one else near them. He spoke in a low voice. "Lloyd George phoned me in the wee hours telling me he received a note. It warned him to accept the peace proposals if he wanted to see his daughter alive. He's beside himself."

"My God! I didn't know that. I told Darnell I'd meet him at Downing at nine. We'll look at it." Her mind raced on. "There are other developments—I haven't had a chance to tell you. Darnell and I think the girl was chloroformed in the basement of Downing Street and pushed out the cellar window to an accomplice. It may have been the escape route for whoever was involved."

"Makes sense, avoiding the household and servants."

She poured her tea into the cup and fastened her eyes on Howard's. "Chief, we need more help, now. This is the biggest case we've ever had. Every Sergeant should be pulled off whatever they're doing and put on this."

Howard scowled. "I'm ahead of you on that. I've been gearing up for it. Now we have that note, we can see the nature of what we're facing. I'll have a meeting this morning while you're at Downing. You'll stay as the lead there, and concentrate from that end. I've got to get the search operation going from here. I'm adding Jenkins and Brooke to search for Megan. They're bloodhounds on a hunt."

She glanced at the wall clock. "Have to go soon. I'll be back from Downing later."

She gulped the last of her tea and hurried to her desk. She was about to leave when a gray-haired woman walked up to her desk and spoke to her.

"Are you Sergeant O'Reilly?" Her voice was tremulous.

"Yes. And you are . . . ?"

"I'm Robert Brent's mother. At Downing Street, they told me you were handlin' the case."

O'Reilly stepped over to her and took her arm. "Come and sit down, Mrs. Brent."

The woman sat in a chair opposite the desk. O'Reilly pulled up another chair to her side.

"I'm sorry to bother you. I . . . I don't know what to do. Robert's father died just a few years ago, and now Robert . . ."

O'Reilly put a hand on the woman's arm. "I'm so sorry about your son."

The woman nodded. "You've got to find him, punish him. If Bobbie, Robert's father, was here, he'd be wild. I'm beat down."

O'Reilly recalled her own feelings of dejection just

an hour earlier going through Brent's things. She could not forget the injustice of the brutal act that cut his life short in a violent end.

"We'll do everything we can, Mrs. Brent. We have our best people working on this and we won't stop . . ." She felt a tear in her own eye and touched it with her sleeve. "We'll get him."

Robert Brent's mother left a few minutes later. O'Reilly sat watching her cross the office to the stairs. She took a deep breath, and scooped up her purse and coat. Time to go. Time to prove to his mother that they could do something about the young man's death.

Five minutes later Catherine O'Reilly's auto was clattering down the cobblestones leading away from the Yard toward Downing Street. She reviewed where she stood in the case. It was getting more complicated, but there'd be plenty of help. Howard's support and control of operations from the Yard to scour the city for Megan with experienced officers gave her confidence. She would not be the only officer with the weight of the investigation on her. And whoever found the girl and Brent's murderer, whoever got credit . . . that didn't matter at all.

With all the help for searching London that emanated from headquarters, she and Darnell could concentrate on the scene of the crime and develop a strategy leading from the house, the séance, and the people who were there. O'Reilly's pulse raced as she plunged into another day.

Chapter 9

The Prime Minister faced John Darnell and Catherine O'Reilly across the desk in his study. "Look at this," he said. He handed them the German note.

They stared at it together. Darnell shook his head and read a few words of it aloud, " '. . . accept the German peace proposals.' Have you read those proposals yourself, Prime Minister? Could you accept them?"

"Read them, yes. Accept them? Not a chance in hell. The other side started this war. Now the Huns want to go back to the status quo, try to keep the land they've taken. Neither England nor France could accept those terms."

Darnell asked, "Our side wants reparations?"

"They want justice, John. Think of all the men we've lost. They want the German imperialists to feel the heel of democracy on the backs of their necks, their faces ground into the dirt."

"That sounds like a good speech," Darnell said. "Will you be saying that to Parliament on the nineteenth?"

"I'll use words like that, if I can—but what can I do?" He raised both arms toward the ceiling. "They have Megan."

"She's a hostage, sir. The ransom, as the Chief Inspector warned, is not money. It's your giving in to their demands."

Lloyd George scowled. "But if I gave in, how would I know they'd return Megan?" He sat, silent, staring into space.

"That's the misery of kidnapping, sir," Catherine O'Reilly said. "In the Danielle case, the kidnappers wanted ten thousand pounds. They knew the mother could afford it, and she would have paid it. Fortunately, we tracked down the kidnappers. We have to find your daughter, too, as soon as possible."

"Kidnapping is a damnable crime," Darnell said and scowled. "If I could get my hands on them . . ." He swallowed hard. "They'll contact the Prime Minister again."

O'Reilly nodded. "Yes. And soon. Perhaps by phone. When they do, he could try a delaying tactic."

"Yes, if they telephone, the Prime Minister could ask to speak to Megan. To make sure she's all right. That would be normal." Darnell looked at Lloyd George for confirmation.

Lloyd George's eyes widened. "Of course I'd want to hear her voice. I wish I could hear it now. But what if they don't put her on, what if she's . . . ?"

"Don't think the worst, sir," Darnell said. "The fact that they sent the note shows that holding her hostage is their best position, from their attitude. Which means Megan is alive and all right."

"What can you tell them about the proposals, sir, if they call?" O'Reilly asked. "Can you buy us some time?"

"Commons doesn't meet for three days, but I can't bear to think of Megan a prisoner that long. Three days! I want her now." His eyes welled with tears, and he paced the floor for a moment. "All right . . . I'll tell them that until I hear Megan's voice, there's nothing to discuss. And that much is true. Then I could say I'm studying the proposals."

Darnell nodded. "They know Parliament's schedule. I think they targeted you for this the minute you became Prime Minister. They knew peace feelers were coming, and you'd have to speak to Parliament on the nineteenth. It was all planned well in advance."

"Planned? A week ahead? But they couldn't have known about the séance. We didn't decide that until the last few days." Lloyd George fussed with a pencil on his desk, snapped it in two. "I'd like to snap their necks—like that!"

Darnell went on. "If the séance hadn't been held, they would have done something else. It was just a fortunate convenience for them."

Lloyd George swore. "How could they dare. In my own home."

Darnell said, "People coming and going. A dark night, cars parked all about, rain, a séance. This all made it possible. The activity and the confusions."

O'Reilly nodded. "They used the séance as a diversion."

"Exactly." Darnell brushed hair back from his forehead. "But, I don't know. That medium. She could actually be part of the plot. And someone in on this knew the home's layout."

"So, two conspirators, one outside." O'Reilly put her notebook into her purse. "Could the medium have organized all of this?"

Darnell shook her head. "She doesn't seem the type, of course. But we can't rule out that possibility. Or anything."

O'Reilly turned to the Prime Minister. "Chief Inspector Howard wants you to know we're putting every available officer on this, sir. Our best men. Our best detectives. He's directing a citywide search for Megan."

Lloyd George sagged in his chair. "So all I can do is wait? Wait for those devils to contact me?"

Darnell said, "If they call, do as we suggested."

"I will."

David Lloyd George rose and shuffled out of the room, hands stuffed deep in his pockets, the habitual sign that showed he was in one of his now even more frequent depressions.

After their meeting with Lloyd George, Darnell and O'Reilly stood on the front steps of Ten Downing Street. O'Reilly said, "Let's talk a minute. There's something else I didn't feel I was ready to bring up with the Prime Minister."

She told Darnell of the deck of cards that had been on Brent's body after he was killed. "What do you think?"

Darnell ticked off in his mind what he thought the card markings could be. "Signs of the zodiac? Fortune-telling cards? Tarot cards?"

"No. Just regular cards. But why would Brent have them, that's my question."

"Maybe they were the medium's. I want to see them . . . Are you going to the Yard?"

"Yes."

"I'd like to see the possessions that were on his body."

"I have to stop at my place," O'Reilly said. "Meet me at the Yard in half an hour."

Fifteen minutes later, Catherine O'Reilly pulled up to the brown brick building in which her flat was located. She quickly entered the lobby and ascended the interior stairs to her third-floor flat.

Uniformed most of the time, she was pleased at being able, at least here, to keep a feminine look about her. Windows were draped with colorful curtains, and fresh flowers stood in vases in each room. The walls of the hallway were adorned with two large mirrors and several family portraits. A gentle incense fragrance still hung in the living room air.

As she walked into the small kitchen, she stopped at a photograph of a gray-haired man standing in front of Scotland Yard. At the bottom of it a small gold plaque read, "Inspector Harrison O'Reilly." She touched it with her lips. "Hello, Dad."

She took down some items from her kitchen cupboard and prepared small dishes. She called out the name of her cat. "Tabby, Tabby." In a moment a large smoke-gray Persian walked with stately steps into the kitchen and meowed. It brushed the Sergeant's leg and purred, looking up at her and at the counter.

"Sorry I forgot you this morning, Tabby. Too busy." She bent down and put the dishes on the floor. "Okay, here it is. It might be another long night."

Five minutes later O'Reilly was rolling toward Scotland Yard in her car.

Darnell sat across from O'Reilly at her desk at Scotland Yard. The office bustled with activity, officers charging back and forth. Chief Inspector Howard had held his organizational meetings and set wheels in motion. O'Reilly set the box of Brent's belongings in front of Darnell, and he examined the contents carefully, holding the deck of cards aside for last. He inspected them. "It looks like the cards are the only interesting thing. I'd like to take them with me and study them tonight."

She nodded. "They're evidence—I'll need them back." She put the box of Brent's effects in a large desk drawer and glanced at a clock. "I have to meet with Howard."

Darnell nodded. "I'm going home to play a little card game." He tapped the pocket where he had put Brent's deck of cards. "It's called 'Break the Cypher.'" After leaving, while driving back to his flat, his mind dwelt on the cards. The mere peculiarity of them made him believe they were important.

Chief Inspector Howard and Sergeant O'Reilly reviewed the case again with the new detectives and other men assigned to it. Howard drew a grid on the map of London for a search of the city by teams of men. That morning, they had put together a list of men and women previously involved with either kidnapping or child molesting, and a second list of pacifists in London who had demonstrated in public against the war, anyone who could have clear motives to write the note to the Prime Minister.

Chief Inspector Howard laid down the strategy, and the teams were rushed out to begin their searches. Scotland Yard's web began to stretch out wide, throughout London.

Chapter 10

Saturday noon, December 16, 1916

Penny met Darnell at the front door of their flat when he returned. "Just in time for lunch." She smiled. "Nice to have you home."

They embraced and stepped into the dining room. Sung was laying out silverware on the table, and the aroma of the lunch buffet dishes on the sideboard wafted through the room.

"If I'm not mistaken, that's a beef stew," Darnell said.

Sung nodded. "Cold day, hot stew."

"One of your favorites, dear." Penny hooked her arm in his and walked him to the sideboard. She lifted the top from one and then the other of the silver serving dishes for him. "I set out some wine."

Darnell sniffed the food. "I haven't had a decent meal with you in a while."

They ate leisurely, enjoying a red wine with the lunch.

Darnell told Sung, "We'll take coffee in the sitting room."

Penny sat on the sofa. "Tell me about your case, John. How are you doing?"

Darnell frowned. "I'm afraid it's bringing back old memories. My brother's disappearance." He paused. "Maybe I'm trying for some kind of redemption in this case, because it's brought back feelings of guilt about that. It's under the surface, but intense. I feel guilty not working on the case right now."

"But why guilt, John? You had nothing to do with your brother's disappearance."

Darnell's eyes moistened. He was surprised at that, after all the years. "It wasn't what I did, more what I didn't do. I just think it was my fault. I guess I've always thought that."

"You were just a boy, dear."

Darnell projected his mind back across thirty years. "I haven't told you much about Jeffrey . . . We always played after school, dawdling on the way home. We liked a stream in the woods across the road. Clear water, rocks making a path across it. We'd walk over the stream on the rocks and back. We'd watch the fish wiggling by. Or lie on the bank and stare at the clouds."

"All boys do things like that. My brother did."

Darnell rushed on. "That day—that last horrible day—I didn't want to go to the stream, I don't know why. But Jeff was stubborn. Said he was going anyway. I couldn't get him to come with me, so I walked slowly down the road, thinking he'd follow me. After a while, I looked back and he was gone. I ran back, but couldn't find him."

"You thought he went to the stream?"

"Yes, I thought so, at first. So I ran there, but found no sign of him. I ran home, thinking he'd slipped by and was already home. But there were horses, buggies, going along the road in both directions. It was a direct route to Cleveland, the biggest city in Ohio, you know, a place that could swallow up a small boy easily. Someone . . . I don't know, the police thought he could have been kidnapped. Someone could have grabbed him not more than a hundred yards or so behind me."

Penny's eyes met his as she rested a hand on his arm. "I know this hurts when you talk of it. You have to find a way to put it behind you."

He put his hand on hers, and exhaled a deep, shuddering breath. "You're right. But that's why I feel so deeply about this case. The bad memories."

She put an arm around his shoulders.

Darnell felt calm and at peace for the moment.

Sung knocked on the open door.

Darnell said, "Come," and straightened his tie.

Sung brought in tea, sugar, and cream, with small sweet biscuits on a plate, and set them on the table.

They drank their tea and munched on the sweets.

"I have to be at my charity in thirty minutes," Penny said. "Alice is picking me up."

"A pity. We could have some time together. Besides, Confucius said, *'Charity begins at home.'*"

"I think you're confusing Confucius with Sung."

Darnell laughed. The easy afternoons with Penny after classes or between cases were the greatest pleasure of his life, even more, he admitted to himself, than cracking a dense paranormal mystery. Often he reflected how much his life had changed since she came into it.

"All right," he sighed. "I have a little project of my own." He pulled the deck of cards from his pocket.

"Solitaire? Now you're trying for my sympathy."

"Not solitaire. More of a mystery card game."

"You can tell me later. I must get ready." She touched her lips to his lightly, then hurried to the stairs.

Some minutes later, Darnell said good-bye to Penny in the entryway before returning to the large table in the dining room. He removed the flower arrangement, sat at the table, and placed the pack of cards in front of him. He stared at the pack and murmured to himself, "All right, what secrets do you hold, my little Kings and Queens?"

He removed the cards from the pack and spread them out on the table. He studied the handwritten symbols in the upper left corners. He dealt them out into separate piles for each symbol.

Shortly, he had all the cards marked with moons together, cards with suns in another pile, groups with each of the zodiac signs, and others with various astrological symbols. "These signs must stand for letters of the alphabet," he said to himself. "Which symbol is which letter—that's the question."

Darnell counted the cards in each group of symbols, some with only one, several more than four. He noted the quantity of cards for each symbol. A thought came, and he hurried to his bookshelves, muttering, "That literary guide to letter frequency. Where is it?"

Locating it, he returned to the table with Lockington's edition of *Bowles' Complete Book of Cyphers* and pored through the pages. In a few moments he found a passage and exclaimed, "Here it is— *'ETAOIN SHRDLU.'* The old printer's order of frequency of use of type. The letter 'E' in most common use, then 'T,' and 'A,' and so on. But will it work on this?"

Sung knocked on the door and stepped into the room. "Do you wish anything?"

"You heard me talking with myself, didn't you?"

Sung bowed slightly. "Who is winning argument?"

"The cards, I think." Darnell smiled and sipped the tea. "Take a look at this, Sung." He showed him the symbols on the cards. "Someone is using what we call a 'cypher,' a code. Now, there are more moons than any other symbol, so they must be the letter 'E.' Then the suns are next, so I'm thinking they would be 'T.' "

"Sound like *I Ching*—Chinese picture symbols. Heaven, earth, thunder, water, mountain, wind, fire, lake. Pictures tell story."

"Right. These cards will tell me a story."

Sung left, and Darnell concentrated on the frequencies. "This is a small universe, one deck of cards," he murmured. "So results won't be perfect." He studied his list. "Damn! I need more to work with." He stared blankly at the small piles of cards and his notepad.

He talked to himself. "The question is, why did Brent have these cards . . . was a message directed to

him? Did he read the message and reshuffle them?
Was he killed because he read the message?"

Darnell threw down his pencil in frustration, stalked
over to the sideboard, and poured a stiff glass of
sherry. He took a gulp as he went over his list and
rearranged the random symbols and letters in frequency order.

Questions jumped about in his mind. Was Brent
going to send the cards to someone? Or did he receive
them, find them? Was he part of the conspiracy? Did
he steal the cards?

The cards themselves, as a device, pointed toward
a medium. They had that flavor. Of course, mediums
used different kinds of cards for telling fortunes. In
this case, he was convinced the message may have
had something to do with Megan's disappearance and
ultimately with Brent's death.

Darnell filled a pipe and puffed, the stem clenched
tightly in his teeth. He made variations of his basic
list but nothing seemed to work, and he felt he'd over-
looked a simple variation.

Suddenly he thought of the *suits* of the cards. In
ordinary playing cards, the suits would have something
to do with the code. He'd have to try every variation
in the order, suit by suit. If his assumption was correct,
he might be able to unravel the message. He moved
cards about and made notes. But thirty minutes later
he heard the knocker on the door resound in the hallway. Sung came to the dining room door and said,
"Man to see you at front door, Professor. From *London Times.*"

Darnell pushed his chair back. "Take him to the
sitting room. I'll be there in one minute."

He turned his notes and the cards facedown on the
table, glanced about the room, closed the door, and
walked across the entryway to the sitting room. He
continued toward the red-haired man standing there
with a notebook under one arm and the other outstretched toward him.

Darnell shook his hand. "Sandy MacDougall. What

brings you here, today? You haven't quizzed me lately. Running short of news?"

The reporter laughed lightly, the event brightening his rather thin and somber face. "With the war on, hardly so. But something has come up, partly dealing with the war, partly a very personal matter."

"Have a seat." Darnell suspected what was coming.

The other settled himself in the large, high-backed chair. "Rumors are rife, Professor, that something bizarre is going on in London. And when the word 'bizarre' comes into play, we think of you."

Darnell laughed. "That's a reputation not many would envy."

MacDougall frowned. "Seriously, the press can't fail to see all the police activity about town. Rousting latent dissidents who might be involved in some insidious plot regarding the war. At the other extreme, hauling in borderline criminals who might be suspected of sex crimes or perversions regarding children. And, then, which is why I'm here now, there's talk of 'séances.' " He kept his gaze focused on Darnell's face.

While Darnell had presumed, merely from the reporter's presence, that he had got wind somehow of something big happening, he was shocked that Mac-Dougall had identified all three critical elements of the case. Fortunately the man hadn't connected them.

"Can you tell me any more about all this?" Darnell asked. "Are you putting together a story?"

MacDougall gave Darnell a wry smile. "That's just like you, answering a question with a question when you don't want to talk. Yes, I'm writing a feature. Maybe three features. I don't know how to tie these different things in. But something's going on, and it's big."

"Have you talked with Scotland Yard? If there's police activity, that's your main source."

"They wouldn't breathe a word. Talked about national security on the one issue, interrogations of men who've shown they were against the war. No comment on the other things."

"I understand the Yard's position. 'We are at war, aren't we?" Darnell thought a moment. "Sandy, listen . . . we've worked together going back to that first case of mine you called 'The Old Bailey Ghosts.' You were always fair, even if a bit sensational. I have to call on your fairness again. Wait until more facts come out. That way, you won't endanger the war effort or any police activity. When you come back to me with your complete story, I'll give you all the information I can, for *The Times.* I've done that before, and you've come out ahead."

"You're saying you are involved."

"I can't add anything to what you know at this time. I just appeal to you to hold off on your stories for a bit. Facts will come to you later."

Sandy MacDougall closed his notebook. "It looks like I'm going to have to commune with the spirits to get any more out of you." He sighed. "All right, I'll wait. But when you tell me the story, whatever it is, I get it from you first, and no one else gets it until *The Times* comes out."

"Agreed." The two shook hands. As Darnell closed the front door after the reporter, he leaned against it and said, "Whew!"

Chapter 11

Saturday afternoon, December 16, 1916

David Lloyd George sat at one end of the long, polished cherrywood dining room table and his wife, Margaret, at the other. Brilliant silver serving dishes sat between them on the long centerpiece velvet table cover. Three candles flickered in the silver candelabrum at the center of the table. A servant stood against the end wall four feet back from the left shoulder of each of them.

"I don't understand it," Margaret said, her voice sounding sepulchral in the huge dining hall. "Why our daughter? Why take such a child?" She kept her voice steady only with great effort.

Lloyd George looked down at his lunch plate, the food untouched after the first taste. He had no appetite, no wish in life except to see his daughter alive again. And he feared that might never happen. But he couldn't let his wife suffer a thousand deaths.

He gestured to the servant to remove his plate. "Bring me a stiff brandy," he said.

To his wife he said, knowing he had to reassure her, "Don't worry, Maggie. She'll be all right. We have the best people on the case."

"But you've said that before, those very words, and what have they done so far? And where is our

Megan?" Tears flowed down her cheeks and she blotted them with her napkin.

"We know she's alive. The note, whatever else it said, told me she's the hostage for my position. That's actually good news, knowing she's being held. *I'm* the one really held hostage. All I have to do is accede to their demands, and she'll be home the same day."

Margaret stared at him. "But I know you, David. You, and your, your principles, your determination to win this war. You'll never give in to the Germans. Even if it means . . ." She burst into tears again.

Lloyd George pushed his chair back and walked the length of the table to her side. He put his arm around her shoulder and consoled her.

"Not this time, my dear. The war be damned. I won't let anything happen to Megan. I swear it."

Margaret reached up and took his hand in hers. With the other, she put the napkin to her eyes again. "Just remember, it's our last daughter, our youngest. My baby."

Madame Ilena Ispenska wore the brightest of her long, flowery dresses and tossed a flowing red scarf loosely about her neck. She had let her hair down to its full length, well below her shoulder line. Rings sparkled on her fingers. She surveyed the overall result in the oval mirror on her dining room wall. Her gypsy mother, she thought, would approve, if she were alive.

The medium inspected the table placement. A single candle burned in a carved wooden holder in the center, flanked by large serving dishes on either side of it containing her specialty, which was a goulash dish in one and a lettuce salad in the other. An open bottle of red wine stood behind the place setting designated for her guest for a late lunch, and a wineglass sat to the right of each of the two plates.

As she examined her handiwork, a light tapping came on the front door and she walked toward it, her hips undulating with the affected walk she had adopted for the occasion. She felt as young as twenty-five again, in those days when she was popular with men, yet she would reach forty before the year was out.

Opening the door, she beheld, with no surprise, the figure of Hugo Stanton, beaming at her with his ivory smile. He stepped through the doorway, pushed the door back, closed it with his body, and took her into his arms. They kissed passionately.

Stanton pulled back. "Something smells very good," he said. "You, of course—but I must say also your cooking. I'm starved."

Madame Ispenska exhaled the breath she was holding. All morning she had thought about their first night together, that night before the first séance, when Hugo unexpectedly came to her house. He had brought new passion to her life that night, and in fact changed her view of what might lie ahead for her. She had not been loved that way by a man for years, since her husband died, and, then to be ravished by such a man as this . . .

She breathed, "Hugo. I've missed you."

"Then let us eat quickly, so we'll have more time together. I can't stay long." He stepped over to the table, picked up the wine bottle, and filled both of their glasses. He held one out to her and took the other.

"To us," she said, and clinked her glass to his.

As if they were magnets, his eyes held hers as they sipped the wine. With an effort, she pulled her gaze away and served the food.

They finished their wine, and Stanton refilled the glasses. They laughed as they ate. Afterward, she set the dishes aside and they walked arm in arm to her living room and the sofa. She pulled him down to her on the sofa and they embraced again. Although Stanton seemed totally in control of himself, Ilena felt herself becoming giddy, in her daze of passion. But with part of her mind, she wondered at the subtle difference in his attitude.

"You do love me?" she asked when Stanton at length pulled back and lit a cigar. Her hands roamed over his muscular arms. She touched his cheek softly.

"Of course. But there are serious matters to consider now."

She felt reality reclaiming her mind. Serious matters. She knew what he meant, but had hoped he would not broach any of it that night to spoil their evening. Now that he had . . .

"I . . . I'm worried, Hugo," she said. "That poor girl, missing, and that young man. Will they blame me?"

"Not unless you have magical powers to make people disappear." Stanton's expression was blank.

She thought the first night had given her a glimpse into his real being, his openness. But now he was holding back.

"We won't talk of it. It accomplishes nothing." He continued to stare at her and exhaled smoke.

She pulled away from him, to the edge of the sofa, and glared as he complacently puffed his cigar. "You know something you're not telling me. Were you involved in . . ."

"Kidnapping and murder? No. And I wouldn't advise you to suggest that to anyone."

"Those words you said to me that first night about us . . . were they all lies?" Her face wore all the lines of her forty years now, girlish dreams gone. She turned away, not wanting to let him see her like that. "Did you make love to me just so I would go along with, with . . . whatever it is you're doing?"

"You suspect me, then?"

"I don't know what to think. I love you, Hugo. But I see you don't return it."

"I've said I do. Do words mean nothing to you?"

"What you do, how you treat me, means more."

Hugo Stanton stood lazily, cigar dangling from his mouth, and raised both hands up in the air in resignation as he walked to the front door. "Too much talk. I must go. I have a lot on my mind just now. But I'll be back later. Meanwhile, don't think too much about all this. And don't talk about it with anyone. I advise you well, Ilena—say nothing to anyone about what you *think* you know. You will regret it."

She held her head high and looked away as she held the door open for him to leave. "I promise nothing."

Penny Darnell returned from her charity meeting for wounded war veterans just before teatime, and joined Darnell in the sitting room. "Finish your card game?" She smiled and embraced him.

He scowled. "No, I just gave up for a while. Where's Sung? Tea's due."

They talked there, awaiting Sung's no-doubt prompt arrival at four p.m. The telephone rang, and Darnell picked it up.

A gruff brogue came over the line. "Conan Doyle here. I've got to get my mind off Downing Street for a while. What are you doing for dinner?"

Darnell fell in with Doyle's mood. "If you're asking whether you can come, the answer is, be here at eight." He glanced at Sung, at his elbow, who had heard. "One more for dinner?"

Sung nodded. "Plenty of fish."

"I heard that," Doyle said. "I'll see you at eight sharp."

"Conan Doyle picked a good night to come," Penny said. "We're having trifle for dessert."

After their tea, Darnell loosened his tie, pulled out the cards, and stared at the pack. He said, "I'll just sit here and think about this card problem for a while."

Penny touched lips to his cheek and went upstairs. Sung cleared the tea serving dishes away, and Darnell retrieved *Bowles' Complete Book of Cyphers* from the dining room. He pored through the pages carefully, and an hour passed quickly. He heard Penny's heels click across the hallway.

Penny stood at the door. "John, time to get ready for dinner. Conan Doyle will be here soon."

He rubbed his chin. "Yes, a bath, a shave, and a change of clothes. That's what I need to clear my head." He walked to the stairs, pulling off his tie and coat as he walked. Penny watched him go, then stepped into the kitchen to see Sung about the dinner.

Chapter 12

Saturday night, December 16, 1916

Darnell walked back down the stairs at just before eight wearing fresh trousers and a deep burgundy-colored suede smoking jacket, a silk scarf loosely knotted into his shirt collar. He stepped into the sitting room, where Penny waited.

She smiled as he approached. "You look like Christmas. And you smell wonderful."

They held each other for a moment.

Penny asked, "What is that scent you're wearing?"

"Musk. Something Sung gave me."

"It's intoxicating." She clung to him.

"You're lovely, tonight," he said, with an appraising look. "Of course, you always are. Just special, somehow . . . I seem to remember that dress."

Penny teased. "How could you not? It's like the one I wore at dinner the first night we met. I found it at Harrod's."

He smoothed his hand over the material. "Nice . . . Yes, now I remember it. It was the violet in the dress matching your eyes that I couldn't forget."

The door knocker echoed in the hallway, and Ho San's light, brisk footsteps soon resounded on the wooden floor. As the door opened, Conan Doyle's voice, directed at the boy, boomed, "Hello, son. Are you the new doorman?"

Ho San said, "Father's busy in the kitchen. I answer door."

"And a nice job of it you do." Doyle entered the room, and he and Darnell shook hands. Penny embraced Doyle's large figure, her arms not reaching around him.

As Doyle took a seat, Darnell presented him with a glass of sherry. "To take the chill off," he said.

Doyle scowled. "The kind of chill I have won't go away."

Darnell nodded. "I know what you're thinking, Arthur."

"Lloyd George is bearing up as well as he can, but Maggie is forlorn. She believes she'll never see Megan again."

"I wish there was a quick solution, but we don't have any real leads. You've seen the note to the Prime Minister?"

"It was definitely German. I spent some time in Germany twenty years ago. I studied in Vienna. Corresponded. I've seen those watermarks. Insidious, isn't it? The writing paper suggests the source is German, without saying it."

Darnell told Doyle about Scotland Yard's search of London. "It's getting some attention. A reporter stopped by to see me, but I put him off."

Doyle scowled. "These séances are having other effects. They've brought back memories of Louise. I have to get my mind off this . . ."

Darnell studied Doyle's somber face. "Well, you can help me later with a little puzzle I must solve."

Doyle's eyes brightened. "I'm intrigued. What is it?"

"After we eat. We'll need the table to work on it."

Doyle rubbed his hands together. "Sounds mysterious. I love a puzzle."

As they ate, Doyle expounded on his favorite subject, his own life, with stories about his cricket and football. He dwelt on his amateur boxing experiences. "I was quite good. Never lost a bout. That may be why they wanted me to referee the 1910 Johnson-Jeffries fight on July Fourth in Reno, Nevada. The fight of the century, they called it. Turned it down. A big mistake. It would have given me a bigger name in America."

Darnell smiled. "You're world famous already."

"Well, I lost some credibility with that idiot, George Bernard Shaw. He blamed the *Titanic* tragedy on Captain Smith. Speeding too fast, ignoring iceberg warnings. The valiant man went down with his ship, what more did Shaw want?"

"The public was happier being wrong with you, Arthur, than right with Shaw." Darnell's eyes twinkled.

"Wrong?"

"Remember, Penny and I were there. We met on the ship, had our first dinner together on it." He glanced at her dress and took Penny's hand in his. "We know what happened, all the ice warnings, the speed, confusion in loading boats, no boat drill."

Doyle scowled. "I still think about that damned Shaw and his articles, his fancy words. He's a petulant pettifogger."

Darnell laughed. "It's time for dessert."

Sung served the trifle, and afterward they took coffee in the sitting room. Penny said she would do some reading. Darnell told Doyle, "I can use your help now."

Back at the dining room table, now cleared, he produced the deck of cards, which he had replaced in the pack in symbol order. He showed Doyle the symbols on the cards, and lists of proposed matching letters.

"A cypher!" Doyle exclaimed, his eyes sparkling.

"I've been using some of the techniques you featured in your Sherlock Holmes story 'Dancing Men' a dozen years or so ago."

Doyle beamed. " 'Adventure of the Dancing Men'— December 1903 *Strand Magazine*. Yes, a nice little puzzle."

"Numerous 'dancing men,' each in a slightly different shape," Darnell went on. "Each one signifying a letter of the alphabet. Quite inventive." He smiled. "I used your technique in working on this, and, of course, Bowles' book."

"Incidentally," Doyle said, "the idea for dancing men came from my stay at Hill House Hotel, near Norwich. In the autograph book, the proprietor's seven-year-old son, Georgie, wrote his signature using little stick-figure men. I used it in my story."

Darnell laid the cards out in front of the author. "See these astrological symbols on the face of the cards? Same idea."

"Symbols used to signify letters. The key in translating them into letters is the frequency of use of symbols."

"Exactly, Arthur. But something's missing. It's baffling."

"It takes time, John." Doyle smiled. "Remember, in my story, Sherlock Holmes worked on it for hours."

They explored various theories, Doyle referring back to elements in his "Dancing Men" story. Minutes clicked on, and an hour, with no progress. Finally, Darnell tossed the cards down. "Enough for now." He pushed back his chair. "Let's try another subject, Arthur. The medium. Madame Ilena Ispenska."

Doyle lit his meerschaum pipe and puffed deeply, exhaling smoke toward the ceiling.

"What do you think? Could she be in league with the Germans?"

Doyle pulled at his mustache. "I don't question her as a medium. But . . . two séances, two crimes. Is it just a coincidence? One has to wonder."

"Could she be holding Megan prisoner at her house?"

He shook his head. "No. Definitely not that. Mediums today conduct most of their séances at their own places. They're too busy to travel to clients' homes. And sometimes, to impress clients, the charlatans of the lot need equipment they keep at their own places. In her small home, clients could hear or see something if she were trying to keep a prisoner there. Also, as a woman . . . could she even manage it?"

"Anyone kept there would have to be bound and gagged?"

"Right. And hidden away all day and night. Not likely."

As Penny stepped into the room, Doyle glanced at the clock. "Time for me to leave." He shook hands with Darnell. "Be on guard," he warned. He tapped the cards on the table with a finger. "Someone's playing a serious game."

Penny showed Doyle out, and returned to the dining room. "Do be careful, John. Conan Doyle's right. I don't like this case. Mediums, séances, kidnapping, a murder. I don't want anything to happen to you."

He pulled her to him. "I'll be careful. You go on up, I'll just stay down here for a bit. Do a little thinking, you know."

After Penny left the room, Darnell glared at the cards. He knew with time so important, he must crack the code that night. He picked the cards up, riffling them with his fingers, and came back to his earlier thought— sort the cards by suit after finishing the letter sequencing.

He listed his most likely sequence of letters next to the symbols on each playing card. He entered "E's" for the moons, "T's" for suns, through the frequency order. Then he penciled in the letters onto the cards. Soon he saw partial words beginning to form in the cards spread out in front of him.

He spoke his thoughts aloud. "The suits now." He moved cards about, placing them by suit on the table. More partial words formed, letters showed patterns. He knew he was getting closer. He put the cards in sequence, Ace to Deuce, and experimented with various orders. Black suits, then red. Suddenly, the words formed from his letters on the cards. He wrote the letters down, spacing between the words as he identified them, and saw the message jump out from the cards—

VITAL HOLD GIRL UNTIL COMMONS
BACK NEW SEANCE BEWARE ISPENSKA

Darnell scowled. " *'Ispenska'*? Did she sign the message—or does it mean *'Beware Ispenska'*?"

He sat back and mused, "So, Brent steals the cards from someone. Who? He sees a code, but can't break it. Then while he's thinking about it, before he can tell anyone his suspicions, he's killed. But who sent the cards and who received them?" He swore.

Darnell realized that, despite Doyle's support of her, his innate distrust of Madame Ispenska had grown. Cards were a medium's tools, he thought. They used Tarot cards to tell fortunes. Cards were the kind of device a medium would think of using. It still could be her, perhaps with an accomplice. In any case, he had to find out.

He glanced at a clock. After eleven p.m. He'd make a surprise visit to Madame Ispenska's house. Despite what Doyle said, he had to be sure whether Megan was there or not. He grabbed his coat and keys, then dropped the cards into one coat pocket and his .38 special revolver into the other.

He scribbled a note to Penny. *"Back soon, important errand, John."* He put it on the table. If she came down, she'd see it.

In minutes, his motorcar was heading down London's dark, deserted streets toward the medium's house. Rain spattered and bounced off the windshield amid sharp thunderclaps and lightning flashes in the sky as the winter storm renewed.

Chapter 13

Saturday midnight, December 16, 1916

As he drove toward Ilena Ispenska's house, Darnell thought about the mysterious medium. Not an older woman, as many mediums were, and with yet a certain magnetism, her deep, dark eyes and long flowing hair, she obviously possessed attributes that might enchant her patrons. He knew the mystique of it all was part of the practice of mental spiritualism.

Spiritualism. There was a power there, he knew, but it was not so much in its trappings, more in the fervor and conviction, even obsession, of those desperate to speak with spirits of their loved ones. He had no belief in it, but understood it. His mother had been drawn to spiritualism in her grief after the disappearance and probable kidnapping of his young brother. Later, she never forgave herself for not trying to reach her own child in a séance. But his father, a preacher, with faith in a universal power, refused to go down what he called "dark paths."

As Darnell approached the medium's house, he throttled the car back and let it coast to a quiet stop at the curb half a block away. He checked to be sure a box of matches and the deck of cards were in one pocket and his revolver in the other. He turned his topcoat collar up and his hat brim down against the rain, but removed his gloves and tucked them in a pocket, in case he needed to use his revolver. He walked slowly toward the house in the light but steady rain. Was Megan held there? He had to find a way into the house without causing alarm.

No lights shone from the windows, nor had he expected any at midnight. The surrounding houses were equally dark, with no sign of life on the street, no vehicles moving, no people in evidence, which was all as he wanted it. He circled the house, observing that the windows were all closed tight. In the back of the house the door also seemed secure, but he saw a door, angled against the ground, that apparently led to a cellar below.

He lifted the door, and in the dim light he could see steep, crude wooden steps leading down into the dark room. He propped the door open with a stick to deflect the rain and allow light from the street. He stepped backward down the ladderlike stairs and onto the cellar's dirt floor. Wispy cobweb fingers touched his face and he brushed them away.

Darnell smiled at the irony of seeing, dimly, in one corner, the visage of a skeleton. A piped contrivance in an open box seemed designed to generate smoke, probably for ghostly effects.

As he inched forward in the semidarkness, he could make out boxes of other implements apparently typical of séances—horns, flutes, cloaks, Tarot cards, white robes, and clear, thin wires. Madame Ispenska, he decided, whether or not she possessed the attributes of a true medium, was clearly prepared to be a performer. Although he hadn't seen her use any of them, he could imagine them creating a magical aura and bringing pitiful shreds of hope to women longing to hear dead husbands or sons speak once more.

Although Madame Ispenska had seemed to talk with the voice of Lloyd George's daughter, Mair, at the séance the night before, Darnell's principles and long-standing beliefs prevented him from accepting it. But was it remotely possible? Did she use the implements, not to bolster her own shortcomings, but to satisfy, for their comfort, those who demanded more than the mere words the medium seemed to produce from the ether? He shook his head. It must be the atmosphere down here, he decided, clouding his thoughts. He moved forward in the dark.

Darnell took careful steps across the dirt floor to a stairwell on the opposite wall. He struck a match and looked up stairs that led to a door. He'd have to find out whether it was unlocked. The match went out, and he struck another.

He took the stairs one at a time, stopping for a minute when they creaked. The doorknob turned easily. He pushed the door open and took one step forward into a dark room that, with a residual smell of cooked food, he assumed was the kitchen.

At that moment, before he could really see into the room, he reeled backward from a stunning blow to his head and tumbled backward down the stairs, his arms and legs banging against the wood all the way to the cellar floor. As his head struck the bottom step, he experienced a bright flash, and his world went completely black.

After an indeterminate time, Darnell came to consciousness, and felt a cold wetness on his forehead. Was it rain? Was he outside? He opened his eyes and saw Madame Ispenska applying a cold cloth to his face. Instinctively, he pulled back. He looked about and realized he lay by the bottom step on the cellar's dirt floor. "What . . . what happened?"

"I hit you. Thought you a burglar. You fell down stairs."

He touched his forehead, and winced. His head, leg, and back ached. He pushed up into a sitting position.

"You hit me, now you're helping me. I don't understand any of this."

"It was a mistake—I am sorry. Can you stand? We should go upstairs. We must talk."

Darnell pulled himself into a standing position with the aid of the stairway bannister. Nothing felt broken,

but his leg ached. He held the cold cloth to his forehead's swollen bruise and followed the medium up the
stairs into the kitchen.

"Come to the table," she said, helping him into a
chair.

He sat heavily and cupped his head in his hands for
a moment. He glanced about. "I could use an
explanation."

She sat opposite him. "I . . . I've had emotional
evening. My friend . . ."

"I have a feeling you won't give me his name."

"I can't. Why are you here?"

"Investigating." He looked about. The place certainly didn't smack of a prison. "The Prime Minister's
daughter is missing, there's been a murder."

"But why my house?"

"You have to realize you must come under some
suspicion. It was your two séances that produced a
kidnapping and a death."

"You thought I held Megan here? You can search."

"Thank you. I will, before I leave." He held his
head in his hands again.

She rose and gave him a fresh cold cloth. She
touched Darnell's hand. "Sit still. I fix coffee now."

Darnell sat watching her move about the kitchen,
preparing the coffee pot, taking down two cups. His
thoughts swirled. Madame Ispenska . . . he had begun
to suspect her—but now?

The medium finished putting the coffee on to boil,
and sat across from him. "I have concerns."

"Concerns about . . . ?"

"These crimes. I had nothing to do with them. Yet
you suspect me."

"We must investigate everyone."

She thought a bit. "You can answer a question,
perhaps."

"A psychic asks a question?"

"It's personal. My friend . . . he changes, I wonder
about him."

Darnell shook his head. "Not part of my expertise."

"No. It's something he said. I want your opinion."

"Go on."

"He told me his mother's side of the family was German."

"And your question?"

"In this war, can a man not a pure Englishman be trusted?"

"He has let you down. You wonder about him now."

"Yes."

"We have many émigrés from other countries. They are not all spies, if that's what you mean."

"In Hungary, where I come from, the attitude is more harsh. My own father was severely treated because of his family."

"If you have anything specific . . ."

She sighed. "Just thoughts, memories of the old country. I have been prisoner myself, in Hungary. It is why I left."

Darnell sipped the coffee. "What do you know about a . . . deck of cards?" He watched her face.

"Cards? Tarot cards?"

He shook his head. Nothing there.

Her dark eyes disturbingly pierced his own. "You come here, you ask questions, you don't trust me. I must prove it. Let me tell you some things."

"What do you mean?"

"You have had a big crisis twice in your life." Her eyes glinted. "Once, when you were very young. The other, in past few years."

Darnell was startled. She was putting on her medium act, looking into his past. He decided to go along with her, test how far she would go. "What do you mean?"

"The first is a relative. A sad parting." She stood and took his hand. "Come with me." She led the way down the hall to her séance room.

Reaching the room, Darnell realized the pain in his leg was greater than he thought, and he sank into a chair at the table. He watched as she clicked on the overhead red bulb, sat next to him at the table, and stretched out her hands to him.

"Take my hands," she said.

He took her hands in his and noticed the cold clamminess of them on this dark, cool night. For an instant he thought of jumping up and leaving, but this might be his last chance to prove her a fraud.

Madame Ispenska closed her eyes and tilted her head backward, face toward the ceiling. Her long hair streamed downward, almost touching the floor. They sat silently, while her breathing gradually became labored and heavy. A low moan escaped her lips.

After a bit, the moan became more audible, taking the form of words, emanating from her lips in a thin, high voice. The voice of a child. It seemed to be a boy's voice.

"Johnnie . . . Johnnie . . ."

Darnell flinched in his chair. It couldn't be . . .

"I've come back . . . to warn you . . ."

Darnell's throat choked up. He wanted to speak, but held back. He would not be a party to the scheme.

"Johnnie . . . they're after you now . . . Can you speak to me?" The small voice came from the medium's mouth.

Darnell clenched his jaw and his grip on Madame Ispenska's hands tightened. He would not give in to this.

"Foreign men . . . cruel men . . . watch out for them . . . I must go now . . ."

Darnell swallowed hard. Was it his brother's voice, that slight, childlike sound? After all these years, how could he be sure? Yet no one had called him "Johnnie" for over two decades. His brother, and his parents before they died, were the last to do it. And the voice sounded like a boy's, like Jeffrey's might, if his recollection of it were accurate. He shook his head to clear away the fuzzy notions.

The medium jerked her hands free and pressed them to her temples. "Oh, God! My head." She opened her eyes. "The room is going around. This is bad."

Darnell rose and turned on a lamp. "Are you all right?"

"Water. I go for water." She rose and stumbled back toward the kitchen. Darnell followed. In the kitchen she quickly drank a large glass of water, then poured another cup of coffee and held it in her hands, looking at the steam rising from the cup.

"Too many years," she said. "Someone comes to me from many years ago. Did you recognize that person?"

Darnell refused the bait. He would not give her that satisfaction. "I have to go now." He pulled on his coat and hat. "May I search your house?"

She scowled. "Of course, if you wish." She took him from room to room and watched icily as he opened all closets and cupboards and looked at objects in the various rooms.

Finished, he thanked her, and said, "At least you know I've cleared you of holding anyone here." As she silently held the door open for him, he strode out the front door, anxious to be in the fresh air. On the front porch he breathed deeply of it. The rain had stopped and the moist, cool air dispelled the unreality of the medium's house.

Darnell drove home in a state of mental and physical exhaustion. The woman must be a charlatan, he told himself, and yet . . . that voice. An image of a smiling seven-year-old Jeffrey flashed in his mind as he remembered the days with his brother, in America. Imagination, he thought, whether the medium's or his own, was a powerful force. A force for good, or for evil.

He knew he couldn't tell Penny of his conflicted feelings, at least not now. He resisted the idea that there was any truth in what he'd heard. But the message he took from it, whether it came from beyond the grave or from the brain of a scheming and devious medium, was very clear. Beware of danger.

Chapter 14

Sunday morning, December 17, 1916

Megan woke and sat up in bed as the door to the attic room burst open. Another morning. How long would she be kept here? Longings for her home dominated her mind.

Slade set a tray of food and drink on the small table. The man's face looked strange this time to Megan. She puzzled about it until she realized he had shaved off his usual dark stubble. The man also wore a clean white shirt and his hair was slicked back. She wondered why he looked different this morning.

"Come, lovey," Slade said. "Breakfast."

His voice oozed a mixture of drunkenness with another emotion Megan could not identify. Instinctively, she shrank back from him, to the far side of the bed against the wall.

"Bacon and toast, girly. And an egg. And milk. Girls like their milk, don't they?" He moved toward the bed.

"I . . . I'm not hungry right now."

"Not hungry? You wouldn't fool a bloke, would you?" He approached the bed and sat down on it opposite her. "And me takin' care of you like this . . ."

He sat on the bed, breathing heavily, leering at her. His voice, harder and throatier, had changed in a way she felt threatened her. "Seein' you lyin' there, with your wavy hair, always watchin' me with those eyes—those big, blue eyes . . ." He reached out and stroked her bare leg.

Megan's eyes widened and her lips trembled. She shook off his touch, folded her arms across her chest, and covered as much of her face as she could with her sweater. "Go away. My father will punish you."

Slade laughed, a guttural sound from somewhere back in his throat, and reached across the bed. "Not bloody likely." He grabbed her arm and pulled her toward him. "C'mere, you."

Megan struck out at his face with her free hand, her fingernails accidentally slashing into his right eye. Slade dropped her arm, and she drew back against the wall again.

"Damn you!" Slade rubbed his eye. "You damn vixen—I'll show you." He jumped on the bed, pressed down on her slim body, and pushed his face on hers. In her fear, Megan did the only thing she could. She bit the rough lips he pressed on hers.

Slade cried out in pain. "Goddammit! You bitch! You're not worth all this." He slapped her across the face. Snarling, he went to the washbasin. He splashed water on his face, and took a mouthful of it. He spat out water and blood into the sink.

"Just go to hell then," he said, and left the room, slamming the door behind him.

Megan closed her eyes and cried. She heard the door lock but did not look up. A vision of her mother's face flashed before her closed eyes. Would she ever see her again? Tears flooded her eyes.

Slade did his best to straighten himself out before returning to the kitchen. Although his lip had stopped bleeding, it was swollen and still throbbed. But as he entered the room, he realized he had no need to worry. Karl was leaning forward on his arms on the table, snoring loudly. Baldrik was not there.

He poured himself a water tumbler half-full of whiskey and took a large gulp. The liquid stung his lip but warmed his throat and stomach. He sat in a chair, tipping it back and resting one foot on the edge of the table. He rocked back and forth as he sipped his drink and thought of the girl. Damn her! All he wanted was to make her feel good. He smirked. All right . . . he'd be honest—he wanted to make himself feel good, too.

Karl stirred at the sound of Slade's chair moving back and forth. "What . . . ? Oh, it's you. Can't we have a spot of quiet?"

"You woke yourself up, snoring." Slade laughed again. "You sound like a pig. Snort, snort, snort." He made the sound for him.

"Shut up . . . Where's the hatchet man?"

Slade looked away from Karl to cover up how, even in his near-drunken state, the words about Baldrik frightened him. He pictured the man with a knife or hatchet, chopping off a finger, a toe, a hand—in his morgue or from a living victim. He had to know more about the man.

"Why . . . why do they call him the hatchet man?" He looked at Karl, putting on a face of interest.

Karl stretched, poured himself a whiskey, and tossed it off neat. "You heard about the morgue. That's true." He looked over at the closed door to the small bedroom and lowered his voice. "Cut off fingers. Mailed them to people." He paused. "The first time I worked with him . . ." He shuddered and took a drink.

Slade said, "Keep going."

"It was something I never want to see again. The old man wouldn't talk, wouldn't tell us where his money was in the big old house." He made a sweeping gesture. "Something like this one . . . Anyway, Baldrik tells me to hold the man's hand down on the table and spread the fingers." Karl looked into Slade's eyes, and gave an evil smile.

Slade saw that Karl was enjoying telling his story, enjoying seeing the fear that Slade knew was now showing in his face. He looked away again, but was mesmerized by the story. "What happened?"

"It was the man's right hand. He was a painter or something, I don't know. Baldrik reached in his back pocket and pulled out his hatchet and brought it down on the man's thumb, right at the joint. The thumb flew up in the air and dropped back on the table." Karl made a sound in his throat. "That was the beginning."

"Beginning . . . ?"

"He took off the little finger next, and raised the hatchet again, the man groaning, saying stop." He paused. "He told us where his money was. Only four hundred quid." He laughed, his gaze fixed on Slade's face. "Two hundred a finger. I got half."

Slade poured another drink. Fear of Baldrik rushed through his body, his pulse racing. He looked at the bedroom door. What if the hatchet man found out he had gone after the girl upstairs? A shiver ran up his back. He was startled by the bedroom door opening. Baldrik stepped in from what was the maid's room, yawning, his arms stretched into the air.

"What a great sight you two are," Baldrik said. "Drunk again? Or still drunk from your last binge?"

The two at the table stared glassy-eyed at him. Slade knew the question had no answer, at least none he could give.

Baldrik said to no one in particular, "I'm going balmy here with you two loonies."

"We get out at night." Karl licked his lips.

"An hour or two with the women. Yeah, if we didn't have that we'd really be crazy." Baldrik walked to the coffee pot on the stove, put his hand on it. "Cold." He lit the gas. "I made the call," he said to the others. "Two more days. Tuesday it's all over. He makes his speech, and that's it. That's our orders."

"And the girl?"

Baldrik smiled with his teeth, but his eyes were cold. "We have to see what the great Prime Minister does first. That's clear, isn't it? I think he'll give in to them."

"And our money?" Karl looked at him.

"We'll get it. He said he'd bring it Tuesday night, after dark. We finish our work here and go our separate ways."

Slade cleared his throat. "Anything happening at their end?"

Baldrik rinsed the coffeepot and filled it with water. He smiled, a humorless one. "A spot of bother with a little stabbing, that's all." Baldrik laughed at his own joke. A dry hack, one loud outburst of sound.

Slade, startled, asked, "Who?"

"A meddler. That's all you need to know. It's all I know. One thing, it'll put the fear of God into the others, especially the PM." He frowned. "But there's one other person that needs a lesson, and I'm told we may have a special job of work tomorrow."

"Your specialty?" Karl asked. "Put a fright in someone?"

"Just put the fear of God in them, yes, or maybe . . ." He let the rest of the words go. "You two want coffee?"

Karl said, "Not Slade. Slade wants to stay drunk." His eyes were in slits, the drink showing in his voice.

"What do you mean?" Baldrik looked at one, then the other.

"Drunk, so Slade can play with his little girl upstairs. The whiskey gets his courage up, if you catch my meanin'."

Baldrik turned around, slowly, at Karl's words, as if he were a panther stalking his next meal, and rested his gaze on Slade. His nostrils flared. "The girl, eh?"

Inwardly, Slade shriveled. He avoided Baldrik's eyes, but glared at Karl. He couldn't let Karl tell Baldrik about the girl. Couldn't think what Baldrik might do to him. He knew the man had his eye on the girl, too—that's why he'd warned them off.

Slade clenched his teeth. "Bugger off, Karl. I'm warning you." Under the table, his hands unseen beneath the oilcloth, Slade pulled his knife out of his ankle scabbard and gripped it tightly. He watched Karl, his mind seething with emotion. One more word by him . . .

Karl looked from Slade to Baldrik, his eyes narrowed, his voice strident, seemingly determined to see Slade shrivel with fear of the hatchet man. "The girl? Ask Romeo—"

His words abruptly became a harsh gurgle as Slade's razor-sharp knife came up from under the table and in one swift motion slashed across Karl's throat, bursting the man's jugular vein and spewing blood across the table.

Baldrik jumped up, brushing at Karl's blood that splattered on his shirt and face. He wiped his face with a handkerchief. "You bloody goddamned fool!" He shouted the words, charged across the room, and landed a heavy blow on Slade's chin. Slade crumpled to the floor, falling into the widening pool of Karl's blood.

Karl lay sprawled on the floor, legs at crazy angles, his hands at his neck, blood spurting between his fingers, his mouth in a grimace of near death, seeming to want to talk. No words came out.

Fists clenched, Baldrik stood over Slade and glared. "I warned you to stay away from the girl." He bent down to Slade, grabbed him by the neck, shook him, as if to pick him up, but then pushed him back down on the floor. "I ought to put you out of your misery, too, you bloody idiot. When the others hear about this . . ."

Slade said, "I . . . I couldn't help myself."

Baldrik's mood changed, his eyes in slits now. "We can make this work for us. I'll talk with Haas. We'll get Karl's share, you and me, and split it."

Slade wiped blood from his face with his sleeve. "What do we do now?"

"Do? Get the damn body out of here and clean up the room. Tidy it up good, and don't take long. We've got a moving chore to do in an hour."

"What'll I do with the body?"

"What do people usually do with bodies, idiot? They bury them. Try the cellar. You'll probably find a shovel down there."

Slade rose, took a seat at the table, and tossed off the rest of his drink. He still held his knife. Until he was certain of Baldrik's intentions, he'd keep it in hand. He wiped the blade clean, still watching Baldrik.

The other smiled at last, a gruesome sight to Slade's eyes, which saw nothing friendly in it. "Anyway," Baldrik smirked, "we get another five hundred pounds to split, matey. A good day's work. I'd say." He slapped Slade on the back and laughed, the sound rumbling, building to a roar, the first time Slade ever heard him laugh that much, the sound all but contagious in its bizarre but deeply frightening aspect. But in between bursts, Baldrik said, "Just keep your hands off the girl. I'm going up to check on her." Then he laughed again.

Slade laughed, too, brokenly, in a flood of relief. But he happened to glance down at Karl and his pool of blood, and felt sick. He ran to the water closet and threw up his breakfast.

Afterward, he sat on the cold floor there, wiping his mouth, and heard Baldrik give out with new bursts of laughter in the kitchen. The sound reminded him of the flocks of crows he used to chase away from his father's crops on the farm. Suddenly he wished he was there, away from all this, back in that other life he once hated, an existence he had considered dull and simple, a life, he realized more and more now, that *was* dull, perhaps meaningless, but at least safe.

Baldrik unlocked the door to Megan's attic room and stepped inside. He saw that the girl was lying on the bed, possibly asleep. Her eyes were closed.

"Hello, girl." He walked to the bed and touched her on the arm. When she flinched and drew back, he knew she was awake. "It's a friend."

Megan opened her eyes and looked up at him

through tears. She sat up in the bed. "Are you taking me home?"

He laughed lightly. "No, little bird. You have to stay here a bit longer. Your old dad has to do a little something, and with you here, he'll cooperate."

"You're just like the other one." Her voice accused.

Baldrik ignored it. "Are you all right? Did Slade hurt you, touch you?"

"N-no, not much. But he was bad."

Baldrik scowled. "He won't do that again, I promise you. Are you eating all right, sleeping all right?"

"I want to go home. Please, take me home."

"Not now." He stood. "In a few days. Just mind your manners, and everything will be all right." He moved to the door and looked back once before he locked it. He could see now what was in Slade's mind. From now on, he'd see to the girl himself. She might learn to like him. And if she didn't . . .

Chapter 15

Sunday morning, December 17, 1916

Returning home from Madame Ispenska's house after midnight, Darnell wearily climbed into bed. Just as he was falling asleep, or just after, he seemed to have a vision or a dream of his brother Jeffrey, accusing him, *"You left me. It was your fault."*

But in the morning, the entire episode of the night before seemed bizarre, unreal, and he could tell Penny none of it. The small voice from the past the medium had seemed to evoke in the séance was still too strong.

He ate hurriedly, downing his coffee too hot, burning his tongue in his anxiety, rushing to leave. He felt guilty taking any time now, even for breakfast, remembering anew how his mother and father and he had felt when Jeffrey disappeared, knowing that somewhere a young girl was in captivity, longing to see her father and mother. And knowing, too, the burdens that rested on Lloyd George's shoulders. He couldn't let them down.

At nine o'clock, he told Penny, "I've got to get back on this case. There isn't much time left." He explained the decision the Prime Minister would have to make on the peace proposals. "I'm going to Scotland Yard."

Penny nodded. "I have plans for later on. You told me to get out." She hugged him and turned toward the stairs. "Will you be able to make it for dinner?"

"No promises. I'll let you know." Darnell picked up the telephone and dialed Catherine O'Reilly's number.

An hour later, Darnell met O'Reilly at Scotland Yard. "We have to go to Madame Ispenska's house," he announced. He described the message on Brent's cards and his encounter with the medium. But he omitted any mention of the séance, and said nothing about what appeared to have been his brother's voice. In minutes they were in his car heading toward her house. He emphasized, "I want to ask her some more questions."

O'Reilly studied him as he drove. "You're sure Megan is not there at Ispenska's place?"

"I looked in every corner." He glanced at O'Reilly across the seat of his car. "Only two days left to find her."

"We're doing all we can. We have eighteen men on it." She surprised him with her next words. "And another woman."

"A second woman? Amazing." He shook his head.

O'Reilly said, "Not so startling. It's Harris. She's very smart. She'll make Sergeant someday."

Darnell laughed. "Scotland Yard in knickers."

She expelled her breath loudly. "You men! Don't you know women are making practically all the war armaments. You couldn't fight the war without us. And we'll be getting the vote soon. Just wait. We've shown we can do good police work."

"I know." He laughed lightly. "Times are changing. Penny reminds me of that, and I see it in the attitudes of my students in my classes."

Darnell shifted subjects. "Have your people come up with any good leads?"

She shook her head, and looked out the window, evidently now lost in thought.

Darnell noticed people in other cars and carriages on the street in their Sunday finery, returning from church services. *If they knew what we know,* he

thought, *would they be so placid?* He glanced at the
silent Sergeant. "Something bothering you?"

"Just thinking. I've had two kidnapping cases. The
first one last year made me a Sergeant. This one—if
I fail—could put me back on a beat."

"Don't worry. We'll find Megan. We're certainly
due for some good news."

He pulled up in front of Madame Ispenska's house.
But the door stood ajar and the drapes were drawn
back on windows usually covered, for privacy or
mood.

"Something odd here," Darnell said.

They stepped up onto the porch with caution, and
Darnell pushed the door wide. No one was in the
hall or living room, and only scattered, odd pieces of
furniture remained. They moved rapidly through the
rooms. No one there, no personal possessions, no
clothing of the medium's in the closets. Bare, the
house still seemed to retain the aura Darnell had observed twice there, of the medium's work, hanging in
the air, in the dark walls and blood-red drapes in her
séance room. A greater chill permeated every room,
not alone from the cool outside air, but from the
darkness of the house itself.

"God," O'Reilly said finally. "It's like a morgue
in here."

Darnell nodded. "A morgue without dead bodies."

She shivered. "Maybe a few ghosts."

He opened the cellar door leading down from the
kitchen, and peered into the gloom. "All her séance
paraphernalia is gone."

They walked back out to the front. Darnell looked
up and down the street. A neighbor, sitting on his
porch steps, stared at them.

"Come on," Darnell said to O'Reilly, and walked
across the lawn to him. As they reached the walkway,
Darnell called to the man, "May we talk with you, sir,
for a minute?" They stopped at the steps.

The gray-haired man puffed on his pipe and nodded
a greeting. "If you're looking for the Ispenska woman,

you're too late. Two men came in a truck this morning, packed her things in it and left." He puffed, and blew smoke in the air. "Good riddance, I say."

"She was here herself, then, this morning?" Darnell and the Sergeant moved up onto the porch.

The man nodded. "Left in a car with one of them. Upset."

"Did you see the man?"

"Two mover chaps drove the truck. You know, young muscles. But they looked more like hoodlums to me. Another one, slick, seemed like the boss, drove the car. He's been here before."

"He was with Madame Ispenska today?"

"He held her arm and put her in the car. Looked like they were having words. They drove off."

Darnell nodded. "Thank you." Whoever had organized the crimes was here, and now he had the medium under his control. Another missing person. Why?

He headed for the car, scowling, O'Reilly at his side, stepping quickly to keep up with his long strides. He spoke with disgust. "Let's go to Downing Street. Doyle will be there. Maybe the three of us can produce one good idea among us. We're at a dead end here."

Prime Minister Lloyd George called his War Cabinet meeting to order at eleven a.m., Sunday, and greeted the members—Curzon, Milner, Henderson, Adler, and Addison, and, attending as an observer, Bonar Law.

"Let's run through the calendar quickly, gentlemen," the Prime Minister said. "I have some . . . special things to tell you about. Addison first. How are we on munitions?"

Addison removed his pince-nez, and stood, surveying the group. "We're keeping up with the demand of the forces now, for munitions, and I'm pleased with that. Women have been brought into munitions production, and over sixty percent of armaments workers are now women. That has boosted output. I'm confident we'll keep our men supplied." He sat down.

Lloyd George called on the next man. "Milner, the sea war?"

"The Huns have a hundred and fifty submarines, concentrating on blocking our food supplies now."

"And doing a damned good job of it, I'd say," Addison snorted.

"We're building our fleet," Milner responded in his gruff voice. "We'll send them to the bottom of the sea, believe me." He paused. "And my trip to Petrograd will help the Russian war effort. We need them to take some pressure off the front."

"Curzon?" Lloyd George stretched a hand of invitation out to his white-haired friend at the far end of the table. Curzon was the oldest of his advisors, worldwise as well as world-weary, and someone Lloyd George knew he could count on for honesty, support, and understanding.

Leaning forward in his usual way on his elbows, Curzon spoke with disgust in his voice. "It's a slaughter, David. Let's not pretend. We mustn't deceive ourselves, or each other, whatever we tell the press." He ran a hand through his thin hair. "Killed, missing, wounded, or captured, we've sustained a million casualties, almost twenty percent of our troops in the field. I say again, it's a slaughter. Like cattle or pigs, not men."

Milner turned to him. "So what do we do? Stop the war?"

"Why not?" Adler said. "Curzon's right. At best, it's just a stalemate. Troops from both sides stretched out in trenches for miles, facing each other across no-man's land. They're ordered to charge, and then cut down by machine guns. Then we send in replacements, and they send in more troops, and it continues. Lambs to the slaughter, I'd say. It's a travesty. Stop it, yes, and save another million men who are still alive."

"Easy to say stop the war, but how?" Henderson's face flushed. "You always seem anxious to criticize the war effort, Adler, at every opportunity. And Curzon's a weak sister, too. If you're such pacifists, why are you on the War Committee?"

Lloyd George rapped on the table. "Gentlemen, gentlemen. I know it's hard on you and hard on the country. But it doesn't help to quarrel. We can see that every day the people lose some confidence in what we're doing because it drags on. But the war has changed. When it began, the war seemed glamorous and adventurous to many. Brothers and cousins joined up together, and marched off singing. Now we have to conscript enough to keep our army up to strength. The public has found out what war really means. They know one out of five men who go to France never come back. They see wounded ones come back, no longer able to fight, hardly able to live. War is hell, even for heroes."

Curzon spoke as Lloyd George stopped. "Excuse me, Prime Minister, but everything you and Adler say is true, and the Germans have an answer to the deadlock. What about their peace feelers?" His chin jutted out.

Lloyd George's voice was grim. "That's what I must talk with all of you about. Despite our desire for peace, we have a greater desire for victory and retribution. Their proposals are insulting. They want us to act as if they were not the ones who attacked the Allies, to simply forget the murder of our boys, the natural result of it, waive any reparations, and give them a moral victory, if not a real one."

" 'Peace without victory,' some call it," Adler said. "But what's wrong with that? Neither side claiming victory. Both sides just calling it off as a bad idea."

The Prime Minister paced back and forth. "What it would really be, Charles, is peace without *honor*," he retorted, in a sharp voice. His emotion triggered his underlying feelings, and his eyes moistened. "There's something very personal affecting me, something I've held back from the public, and from you."

The men's eyes all fixed on him. He knew that Law

and Adler knew exactly what was coming because of their participation in the séance the night before. They, and the others, sat quietly.

After composing himself the best he could, Lloyd George rubbed his forehead and said in a choked voice, looking from one to the other to them, "My daughter, Megan . . . she's been kidnapped."

"Oh, my God!" Curzon said. "The poor girl."

Lloyd George continued. "She was taken out of my own home. The next night, my secretary, Brent, was stabbed to death."

The cabinet members sat staring at Lloyd George. Adler and Law exchanged glances. Law unobtrusively held a finger to his lips and Adler nodded.

Curzon broke the silence in an angry, growling voice, "It's outrageous! Kidnapping, murder. Your daughter, is she . . . ?"

Lloyd George held up a piece of stationery. "She's alive. I know that much. I received this note from her captors. The note says, if I don't approve the German peace proposals, I'll never see Megan alive again." His voice broke, and he slumped back in his chair.

Bonar Law stood. "Damn! What can we do to help?"

"Not much. I know you're all shocked. We had to keep this all under wraps. Mostly, I wanted you to know what I'm facing as I speak to the House of Commons when it reconvenes. Just two more days. I don't have any stomach for accepting the peace proposals. We have to defeat the Germans soundly, or we'll just have war again in a decade or two. It would only put off the inevitable if we settled now."

"But your daughter . . . ?" Curzon asked. "You have another reason to end the war now, a valid one, certainly, to save your daughter. No one could blame you on any grounds."

Lloyd George shook his head. "No, I can't in good faith approve the proposals, even if my daughter's life is at stake. That's my dilemma. Damned if I do and damned if I don't. But, whatever I say on the nineteenth, I ask your support."

"I'm sure Scotland Yard is searching for Megan," Milner said. "Surely they can find her in time."

"I pray so. We have the best investigators on it." Lloyd George said nothing about the séances. Two knew already. He had to hold it to that as long as he could. Soon, he knew, he'd have to divulge his dabbling in spiritualism. The dark thought that recurred in his mind came again. Would he have to resign when that bizarre information became public? That was seeming more likely. He stood wearily, letting them know the meeting was over. Each one shook his hand, offered best wishes and prayers.

Turning back at the door, Lloyd George said, "National security, men, and my daughter's life, depend on your keeping our talks on this in confidence." His face clouded, and head down, his hands deep in his pockets, Lloyd George left the War Office.

He felt depressed, yet relieved to have the ordeal over, his last official meeting until Commons resumed. Now he could return home and see if Darnell or Scotland Yard had any news. Maybe he would hear from Megan. He quickened his step.

Chapter 16

Darnell and O'Reilly reached Downing Street at noon, just as the Prime Minister's car pulled up. The three walked to the door together.

"I've been told Conan Doyle is here," Lloyd George said. "I hope someone offers some hope, some ideas."

Darnell nodded. "We'll want to see some of your files."

They continued to the Prime Minister's office. Doyle, waiting in the hall, stood as they approached. In his office, Lloyd George gestured at a bank of several wooden cabinets. "My files. You can look at everything except the top two drawers, which are locked. War secrets."

Doyle said to Darnell, "You say the medium has vanished, too?"

"Yes. I suspect that whoever is holding Megan has Madame Ispenska at the same place," Darnell said.

"Two days to find them," O'Reilly said. "The searches by the Yard sweeping London, looking at known child abusers, haven't turned up anything."

Darnell said, "We need a new approach. It isn't child abuse, as such. It's a political conspiracy." He turned to the Prime Minister. "If we may, your files on all your staff and all your ministers, files on war efforts, peace proposals, and espionage efforts."

"Some of those on war issues and plans are private. I'll give you what I can." The Prime Minister pulled out several folders from his cabinets and stacked them on a conference table. "You have almost everything out here now except our roster of ships, planes, troop placements, and actual battle plans."

"You take the War Cabinet and peace proposals, Arthur. Sergeant O'Reilly, if you'll scan the espionage reports, I'll look at the staff and ministerial files. Then we'll exchange them. We're looking for a common denominator, some connection. Anything at all."

The Prime Minister ordered coffee and tea brought in, and the three studied the files for over an hour. Darnell was engrossed in what he read, and the coffee grew cold in his cup.

After a bit, he sat back and looked up at the others. "The background on the younger people, Brent and Stanton, is slim," Darnell said. "Brent's father was a cabbie."

"I know," O'Reilly said. "His mother came to see me."

"Good English stock. I'm sure you did what you could for her."

He looked at his notes. "Stanton's father had some government service. His mother was an import. Married and settled here, had the one child."

Doyle asked, "David, how well do you know the people in your cabinets? Especially your War Cabinet."

Lloyd George frowned. "Curzon, of course, is my old ally, the oldest advisor I have. Together, he and I have gained a lot of gray hairs—white in his case. Henderson's very stable and loyal. Addison is as solid gold as his glasses frames. Adler's outspoken, often disagrees with me on issues, independent, a valuable sounding board. Milner's a bit rough-edged, but very competent and persuasive. Bonar Law is my close friend and compatriot. Fights all my battles by my side. All my men are above reproach. I have no reason to suspect any of them, in fact."

"The two who attended the second séance?"

"I asked Adler here, knowing he'd be independent, judging what he saw. And Bonar Law. Well, he's above question."

"This file shows some of your men have large real estate holdings in London," Darnell mused. "Land, homes, a number of rental flats. Do you have any more details?"

Lloyd George shook his head. "Just what's in the file." He stood up and paced back and forth. "Now, listen, I can't believe any of my men are in on this. If you want more details on them, I could ask them in, let them speak for themselves."

Darnell shook his head. "No. And don't ask them anything. Let us do the investigating." He turned to O'Reilly. "The war is the issue here, and the War Cabinet is right in the middle of that. We need to explore their backgrounds, but do it discreetly and quietly. Can Scotland Yard do that for us?"

"With enough time, yes. I'll start this afternoon, but it may take some time. The monetary side is easiest— balance sheets, holdings. Personal philosophies is something else."

Doyle held up the file he had been reviewing. "There are references in here to the German embassies and officials who worked there before the war. It reminds me that I know a young man who might help, Alfred Sheinhofer. He had a German father and an English mother."

"How do you know him?" Darnell asked.

"I knew his mother. She was an Englishwoman who married a German and moved to Germany. Alfred was born there. He's a fairly young man. I met him in Germany before the war, in my travels there. I heard he fled to England when the war started. This file shows that he works for the War Office now, in the counterespionage section. When I knew him, he had some connections with the German Embassy."

"An odd job for a half-German to be in the War Office. His name alone sounds suspicious. But if you think he can lead us anywhere in this, it's a chance."

Darnell pushed his chair back and stood, feeling nervous energy flowing, eager to get on to the chase. "We have to consider anything."

Doyle went on. "Alfred knew some of the German Embassy staff."

"The embassy could be a tie-in. Remember that note the Prime Minister received? It could be on writing paper from the embassy. Locate him, Arthur, if you can. Let's try to see him tonight." He paused. "But, remember, Sheinhofer could have written that note himself."

The older, heavyset man in the dark corner of the room stared contemplatively at the other, across the desk. His face was half-hidden in the darkness. He riffled a deck of playing cards in his hands. "Well, Haas, you took the medium, then?"

The man he called Haas squirmed. "Yes, I have her, and moved everything out of her house, just as you ordered. But why? What good will she do us?"

The other smiled crookedly. "None at all. That's exactly it. She's served her purpose. Now she can be nothing but a danger to us." He rubbed his chin. "Best we keep her out of circulation."

"I don't like the way this is going. I have to deal with those idiots you gave me. Just two left now. One of them killed the third man and they had to bury him in the cellar of the house."

The heavyset man's face flushed. "The body will have to be moved, when this is all behind us."

"The second death. Not a big loss, that one. But Brent? Is that kind of bloodshed necessary to get what you want? I hope nothing happens in this escapade you ordered for today."

The other made a guttural noise. "You're too squeamish. I'll handle that myself. And it's not what *I* alone want in these things. The orders came . . . well, you know where they were sent from. Let us say, from the town where your forebears live."

Haas cringed. "You promised they'd be safe."

"Of course they will. Of course. Soon, this will be finished. The war will be over, and you can go visit them, see for yourself."

"I hope you're right." He paused. "My neck's on the chopping block here."

"We all take risks. War is not berries and cream. Just carry out your end of it. Two more days. And look on the bright side. You'll be a hero there, no matter what you're called over here. You can move there and live in comfort, a hero's life."

Haas looked at the older man in the darkened part of the room. "One murder already, and the kidnapping. Heroes are soon forgotten. Traitors are hanged."

"Then whatever happens, you won't suffer long. Either in your fame, or your infamy."

Chapter 17

Sunday afternoon, December 17, 1916

Penny Darnell's heels clicked on the hardwood floor as she hurried to the door of their flat. "I'll get it, Sung," she said as he approached also, from the kitchen. "I'm expecting Alice Woodley."

Opening the door wide, she greeted her friend with a broad smile. Their charity work gave them a common bond, but this was a different expedition. *"Entrez-vous, madame,"* she said. "Ready for our adventure?"

"Let's go. My car's purring." She nodded at the roadster.

Penny glanced outside. "It's cloudy."

"The top's up. Just bring a good wrap."

Two minutes later they were motoring along Kensington High Street. "I'm amazed at you, Alice. You can drive on the wrong side of the road, with the wheel on the wrong side of the car. This is a *'through the looking glass'* world."

Alice laughed. "Still an American by habit. Get a driving license. You'll learn the new way. Driving is fun."

Penny shook her head. "So, this war charity event at Madame Tussaud's should bring in a lot of money. Buy a lot of bandages and hospital equipment."

"Right. We're all excited about it. Many important people will be there. With important bank balances."

Penny laughed. "That museum is such a tradition here, isn't it? I've never been there. Wax museums have a reputation, you know, for displaying the gruesome side of life—killers and so on."

"We'll be safe." Alice laughed. "They're all made of wax."

Penny sat back and relaxed. She glanced at Kensington Gardens, Albert Hall, and other familiar buildings they passed, not really noticing them. Her mind was filled with thoughts of John and the Lloyd George case.

"So," Alice asked, "John's on another eerie case, chasing ghosts?"

"I can't talk about it much, Alice. But, yes, something like that." She frowned. "I always worry about him, you know. I know I shouldn't." She looked at her friend. "It's silly, isn't it?"

Alice rested a hand on Penny's arm. "Don't worry. John can take care of himself." Shortly she said, "First the wax museum, then lunch."

Reaching the museum, they parked around the corner and took their places in the line of well-dressed men and well-gowned women. They presented their invitations at the door and said hellos to the attendants and other members of the charity group. After the pleasantries, they passed through the entrance and Penny found herself standing inside a dimly lit hall, surrounded by wax statues of kings, queens, heroes of all kinds, and beautiful women from all the ages.

"Look! Sherlock Holmes and Dr. Watson," Penny said.

"And Queen Victoria."

They strolled through the gallery, moving along with the general flow of the small groups of people passing through. Penny marveled at the accuracy and realism of the wax portrayals.

"Tourists love this place," Alice said. "It's a combination of a bit of history and a spot of the macabre.

Wax museums are always spooky. Tourists expect that. They like the chills."

"I feel like a tourist myself." Penny smiled. "I've been a Londoner for four years, but I'm just getting used to this town."

"Do you miss America?"

Penny shook her head. "I have John. And one of my aunts lives up near Southampton. She visits sometimes. That helps."

Time slipped by as they strolled along with the crowds of men and women, inspecting the exhibits. The aura of the rooms became darker and more subdued as they approached a special area.

"This is Killer's Row." Alice pointed. "That's 'Jack the Ripper.' " Alice smiled. "They had to invent his face, of course. No one knows who he was."

"They could never catch him?"

"Well, actually, he just stopped killing. They don't even know what happened to him. He could still be alive."

Penny shuddered. "Let's find a restaurant. I've seen enough."

Outside the museum, Penny gestured down the street and whispered, "Did you see those men?"

Alice looked where Penny pointed. "What men? And why are you whispering? We're not in the museum anymore."

Penny looked again and said, "They're gone now." She frowned. "They were inside. It was odd. Two of them just didn't look like people who would donate to a charity. More like, I don't know . . . maybe sailors. They were never far from us. The other one was well dressed, but, strangely, seemed to be talking to the others inside, and looking at me. I'll never forget his face. Something about his eyes."

Alice looked up and down the street. "I don't see them. Coming out of that Killer's Row, you're probably letting your imagination take over. I feel the same way. Those statues give me the shivers, wax or not. But, here's Crystal's Tea Palace. Let's go in."

Penny surveyed the street a last time. "No odd-looking men in sight."

Inside, they took seats by the window.

"Tea?" the waitress asked.

"Strong tea. And sandwiches," Alice said. They placed their orders.

As they ate, Penny noticed her friend peering out at the street. "Alice, it's all right. I must have imagined it."

Alice laughed. "Then I'll forget it, too."

After lunch, driving home, as they neared the Darnells' flat, Penny said, "You can drop me at Millicent's house. I need to borrow some sewing patterns." They said good-bye at the curb in front of the flat.

After a few minutes at her friend's house, Penny left with a package under her arm. Amid the heavy black clouds, rumbling sounds of thunder, and scattered drops of rain that began to fall, she found herself one of only a few people on the street, with none in her immediate area.

Penny looked up at the clouds and walked faster, hoping she'd be able to reach home before the downpour started. She turned up her collar. Now she saw no one in the entire block ahead of her.

Suddenly two men grabbed her, reaching out from the edge of a building at an alleyway as she passed it. Her parcel fell to the ground. One of the men pressed a hand roughly over her mouth and his other hand around her neck. The second man held her arms as the two men dragged her into the alley.

Penny tried to scream, but the hands of the man behind her tightened on her throat and mouth. She could scarcely breathe.

The second man stood in front of her and twisted both of her arms together, holding them within one of his large hands. He wore a black knit cap pulled down completely over his head, and his eyes peered out from ragged holes crudely cut into the cap. He wore a black jacket, and she thought of the two sailors she had seen. Penny could smell the scent of whiskey on his breath, and the sharp stench of perspiration from his body.

"All right, dearie," he said. He pulled out a long, sharp knife. "You see my friend, here?" He drew the back side of the knife along her cheek. "The other side of my knife—now that's the interesting side, the business side. Do you understand?" His voice sounded malevolent and suggested a coarseness blended with a sly, evil humor of his own, as if he enjoyed what he was doing.

Penny nodded. Her pulse raced and her throat felt tight.

"We may have some business with you again, my friend and me." He pulled the back of the knife slowly across her upper lip and laughed, a blast of stale breath on her face.

"Now, there's a little something I want you to tell your hubby, the great professor. Listen close. If he stops what he's doing, stops all this snooping, my friend and I won't bother you. But if he doesn't stop, well . . . you just don't want to know what'll happen, do you?"

The first man spoke from behind her. "We're going to leave you now, luv. Don't scream, or we'll come back and give you a souvenir you bloody well won't half forget."

The other held his knife in front of her eyes. "Remember my friend." He jammed a heavy black knit cap down over her head and eyes. "Just keep this on your head until you count to sixty, nice and slow. We'll let you loose now, but remember this. No screaming, and count slow." He took his hand away.

She made no sound, but gasped for air, and took a deep breath into her mouth through the cloth cap.

The other man pushed her down into a sitting position on the ground and said, "Stay there." Penny's head hit the wall as she fell, and it stunned her. She felt faint and dizzy.

Through her haze, she heard the sound of running feet. After some moments, she pulled off the knit cap and glanced around. She stood up, leaning against the brick wall for support, and rubbed her arms to restore the blood flow.

She looked down the alleyway, but saw no one. Trembling, she grabbed her purse and package and stumbled out onto the street.

On the deserted street, with heavier rain starting to fall, she hurried toward their flat. Running and stepping down from a curb, she slipped and broke her heel. "Damn!" She sobbed, and picked up the heel. She hobbled home on the heel-less shoe.

At their flat, she punched the doorbell several times, pounded with the heavy brass knocker, and fumbled for her key in her purse.

The door opened and Sung stood staring at her. She burst into the hallway and cried, "Close the door, Sung! Quickly. They may be out there."

Wide-eyed, Sung scanned the street quickly, then closed and locked the door.

Penny reached past him and threw the second bolt on the door. "Is John here?" She pulled off both shoes and dropped them.

Sung shook his head. "No. Not here." He looked at her with concern, and took her purse and package from her hands. "Your head is bleeding, Mrs.? Can I help?"

Her voice broke. "Oh, God, Sung! Two men attacked me! They threatened me. I-I'm not hurt badly, but, oh, Sung, it was horrible! I have to find John. I need him here."

She dropped the knit cap, and ran past him up the stairs to their bedroom. The oily, gritty taste of the man's hand was still on her lips, and she could still feel the imprints of his hands on her mouth and neck. Penny shuddered, and a feeling of nausea rose up in her throat. She gagged on the harsh and bitter taste, covered her mouth and ran into the bathroom.

Lloyd George's butler entered the room after knocking on the door discreetly and waiting to hear the Prime Minister say, "Enter."

"A telephone call for Professor Darnell," the butler said. "It's Mrs. Darnell."

Darnell said, "I'll take it on that phone."

In the library, he picked up the receiver in one hand, the phone in the other, and said, "Hello, darling."

Her trembling voice told him at once something was amiss. "John, some men, they attacked me. They threatened me with knives, on my face. Come home, John!"

"Knives! Were you hurt?"

"No, I'm all right. But I need you."

"Is Sung there?"

"Yes."

"Keep everything locked up. I'll be home as fast as I can."

Back in Lloyd George's office, Darnell announced, "I must leave. I'll talk with you later tonight."

Doyle stood and looked at him. "Is everything all right, John? Anything I can do?"

"An emergency at home. Find your immigrant, Arthur. And, Sergeant, do the best you can with that list of the War Cabinet's holdings."

He whirled and strode toward the front door. In minutes his motorcar was rumbling toward their flat. The late afternoon rain continued, but he left the windows open, the fresh moist wind whistling through the car. He thought the invigorating air would clear his mind. Penny in danger. He needed to do something about that, and without delay.

Arriving home, he bolted up the front steps to the door and unlatched it. An inside chain secured it, but through the opening, he saw Sung approaching. The valet slipped the chain free and Darnell rushed in. "Lock it again. Where's Mrs. Darnell?"

Sung looked toward the stairs. "In bedroom."

Darnell took the stairs two at a time and swept Penny up in his arms as she rushed forward to greet him. He stepped back and looked at her face. He examined her arms. "I can see where he grabbed you, you're bruised," he said. "What happened?"

She took a deep breath. "Two men, sailor types. They had knit caps over their faces, a cutout for their eyes. One put the back side of a knife to my cheek and scraped it across my face. They pulled a cap down over my head and ran off. In a minute, when I thought they were gone, I ran home."

"Did they say anything to you?"

"Just . . . just that if you didn't drop the case you're on, they'd be back." She shuddered. "One said he'd do something to may face. With his knife."

Darnell pulled her close again, and stared at the wall behind her, thinking. His decision came fast.

"Pack some things, Penny. Enough for several days. I'm going to get you somewhere where'll you'll be safe."

"Where?"

"It's better no one knows. Not even you, for now. And I don't want to endanger Sung with that knowledge."

He stepped to the closet and pulled down a suitcase, dropped it on the bed and opened it. "You pack. I'll talk with Sung for a minute." He stepped over to the door, glanced back to see her pull open a dresser drawer, and hurried down the stairs.

He found Sung in the kitchen. "I'm taking Mrs. Darnell to a safe place. I'll be home later tonight. Lock up well, all the windows and doors. Just leave the chain off the front door. I'll let myself in. If Doyle or Sergeant O'Reilly should call, find out where they can be reached later." He paused. "I want you to know there could be some danger, Sung. Be careful for yourself, and for Ho San. You'd better accompany him when he goes out, take him to school and back yourself for the next few days."

Sung nodded. "Where do you take Mrs.?"

"It's better you don't know, Sung. We'll be leaving in a few minutes."

"I will be careful. You, too, Professor."

Darnell put his hand on his valet's shoulder. "We've been through a lot of danger before, you and I. But we have others to protect, now. My wife, and your son."

"Yes, sir. I watch over Ho San carefully."

"I'll see if Penny's packed."

He strode back to the stairs and again took them quickly up to their bedroom. Penny stood at the door, a closed suitcase at her feet, a coat on her arm. She took his hand and squeezed it, and he picked up the suitcase. They went down the stairs together.

At the front door, Sung opened it, bowing slightly. When they stepped outside, Darnell waited on the landing until he heard Sung lock the door behind them. Then they hurried to his car.

Chapter 18

Arthur Conan Doyle regarded himself as something of a detective, rather in the mold of his created hero, Sherlock Holmes, and he had some cause to claim the distinction. On more than one occasion, he had inquired into unusual cases in England where he believed in the innocence of a man wrongly accused of a crime, and helped to clear the man's name after some painstaking investigation.

This night, Doyle saw his mission to be more simple, if no less urgent. Find Alfred Sheinhofer. He called in at the government agency where the man worked and, with the introduction he took from Lloyd George, was able to secure information from Sheinhofer's file. The address was scratched out, the man had moved, and no forwarding address was shown.

"He won't be in the office for a week," the secretary said. "He's moving."

"We can't wait that long," Doyle said. "Give me something, man." With difficulty, he pried from the memory of the secretary the name of the street and boardinghouse that was Sheinhofer's destination, and drove there, arriving at almost seven P.M., just as a moving truck turned the corner, leaving. Doyle bounded up the steps, breathless, and caught the door before it closed, and spotted Sheinhofer just entering his room down the hall.

"Alfred!" he called, and ran forward as the man turned toward him. "Alfred Sheinhofer."

"Dr. Doyle. *Mein Gott!*"

Doyle smiled. "Watch your German or you'll be pinched."

"Come in, come in," Sheinhofer said. But he looked up and down the hallway before he closed the door.

Inside his room, he turned to Doyle and held out his hand. "I don't see you for two years. And then you show up on my new doorstep as soon as I move in."

Doyle shook his outstretched hand. "I need your help, my friend."

Sheinhofer's forehead creased. "My help? Really? You know, I'll do anything. You are in trouble?"

"No, but the Prime Minister needs information you may be able to provide."

Sheinhofer sank into a chair. "The Prime Minister? Me?"

"I can't explain in detail now, but you must come with me tonight. It'll take a few hours. The information you may have could help us immensely. I'll take you to meet someone. We'll tell you all about it there."

Sheinhofer pulled on a coat hanging on the back of the chair. "Then I am ready. You lead the way, Doctor. I help in any way I can."

Doyle shepherded him out to his car and drove off. Within the half hour, they arrived at the Fox and Crow, a building with cross-hatch windows and mahogany front trim, the sign swinging on chains above the door depicting a reddish-brown fox and jet-black crow, the name in ornate script. "Come in, Albert. We'll order a couple of pints, and I'll make a call or two."

The pub buzzed with the conversation of the locals. A dart game was in process at the far end. They took a table, ordered drinks from a white-aproned waiter, and Doyle went to the phone.

He spoke to O'Reilly first, then called Darnell's home.

Sung said, "Professor not home yet. Expect him after a while."

Doyle was disappointed that Darnell was not home, but gave Sung the pub's location.

He rejoined Alfred Sheinhofer at the table. No one sat at the table on either side of them and they had a degree of privacy.

"Someone else will join us soon. We'll do some catching up over a pint."

Sheinhofer smiled. "That's one thing Germans and Englishmen both have in common, a taste for beer and ale. And I'm half and half."

Darnell drove through the light rain to a train station. During the trip, he scowled as Penny told him about her experiences at the museum, describing the three men she saw there, two of whom were the assailants later. "They were stalking you," he said.

He found a spot to park. At the ticket window, he bought a round-trip ticket to a town near their country home in the Cotswolds and placed it in Penny's hand. "You'll need to stay there until I'm sure it's safe for you to return. I'll call the caretaker and have him pick you up at the station."

"John. Now I'm getting worried about you." Penny's forehead wrinkled.

"I'll take care of myself. With you safe, I can concentrate on this thing. Better for both of us." He took her arm and picked up her suitcase. "We'd best hurry, the train leaves in twelve minutes."

In short order, they found the railway carriage and her first-class compartment and he set her case inside. They stood close together on the platform by the open door.

Darnell wiped a tear from Penny's eye. "You're not going to bubble up, are you?"

She shook her head. "I miss you already. You'll call me?"

"Of course I will. Tonight, after you're settled in the house, call Sung and let him know you've arrived at your destination, but remember, don't tell him where you are. I'll call you later."

"Don't make me worry, John. Stay in touch with me."

He gave her a reassuring smile. "I'll call you often."

They held each other close and kissed lingeringly. Darnell helped her up into the compartment. When he closed the door, she leaned down from the window and took his hand. The whistle sounded, and the voice of the conductor came, "All aboard."

"Good-bye, John." Penny looked deep into his eyes. "Do you realize we haven't been apart overnight, ever, since we married?"

"I know," he said. "But this will all be over in two more days. I'll drive up and we can spend time there together."

The whistle sounded again, and they heard the sound of steam released at the engine. The wheels turned slowly.

"Be careful, Penny." Darnell held her hand through the open compartment window until the train's movement slipped her fingers away from his. He watched the train chug down the track.

Penny waved to him just before the train turned out of the station in a long sweeping arc. He could see her no more.

Darnell let out a deep breath, and turned back to the station. He'd call Sung and see if Doyle had any luck finding his friend.

The man they knew only as Haas sat across the kitchen table from his hired thugs, now, with Karl gone, only two of them—Baldrik and Slade. Haas drank Scotch from a water tumbler, his third of the night. He was conflicted as he thought of the woman. Getting even with the Brits, finally, for all the trouble they'd given him and his family was good. But her?

"Foreigners," people had called him and his mother,

because she was from Germany. Didn't they know Queen Victoria was the German Kaiser's grandmother? And George V his cousin? Even the Russian Czar was related to them. He shook his head at the confusion of relationships and why he should have suffered.

Haas's bleary eyes fixed on Baldrik. "So, you put the fear of God into her, then?"

"Fear of God?" He laughed. "Not half. More like, fear of me. She doesn't want her pretty face carved up like a sausage."

"She'll tell her hubby," Slade said.

"She's already told him," Haas said.

Baldrik raised his eyebrows. "How do you know that?"

The other showed his teeth, a jackal guarding his haunch of meat. "I have my ways. I know what they're up to." He guzzled his drink. "You're not my only . . . assistants."

"Hah! I like that word. Assistants." Baldrik's laugh bounced off the walls. He slapped Slade on the back, who drew away from him. "Hello, assistant." And he laughed some more.

Slade scowled. Haas saw the young man recoil at Baldrik's touch. It was understandable, given the other's reputation for enjoying mutilations he reportedly performed with a certain regularity on those unfortunate enough to cross him.

"Down to business," Haas said. "Two more days now. You'll have to keep the girl and woman here until we're told the Prime Minister accepts the peace terms. Then—well, we'll see."

Baldrik glared at Slade. "And keep your buggery hands off the girl. If I hear you've touched her . . ." He let it drift.

Haas said, "Enough of that. And watch yourself now. They're searching for her, and for us. Stay out of sight."

"What else can we do?" Slade glared at Baldrik.

"Cooped up in here with him, twenty-four hours a bloody day?"

"You want some excitement?" Baldrik's eyes narrowed. He took out his knife, snapped the blade open, and scraped the back side of it along Slade's cheek. "My little friend, here, can liven things up for you."

Slade pulled back, eyes wide. He rested his hand on the scabbard attached to his leg under his pants.

"Any more fights," Haas interrupted, "and you'll both forfeit the back half of your pay. And Karl's. Don't forget that bonus."

"Yes, Boss." Baldrik smiled, with his teeth, although his gray eyes were cold and steely. "We're just your 'assistants.'" He laughed again, but the sound came out harsh, raspy and devoid of humor.

Chapter 19

Sunday night, December 17, 1916

Darnell called home from the station and received the message left with Sung to meet with Doyle at eight P.M. He glanced at his watch. Six-fifteen. He decided to hurry by his home on the way. At his flat, he exchanged his coat for a black leather jacket and stuffed his .38 special revolver in one pocket and a small electric torch in the other. It could be a long night and anything could happen.

"Mrs. Darnell will call you, Sung. She'll say she's arrived and is all right. You don't need to know where she is."

"I understand."

As Darnell drove toward the pub where he was told to meet Doyle and his friend, he tried to regroup his thoughts and prepare for the events of the night. He knew each night, each hour, could lead to an abrupt conclusion of the case. He wondered what Doyle's friend could tell them.

He reached the Fox and Crow before eight and found Doyle inside at a table with a stranger, a man in his late twenties.

"Another pint for my friend," Doyle called out to a waiter, and introduced Darnell to Alfred Sheinhofer.

Darnell glanced about the uncrowded room. The early drinkers had gone home for their Sunday dinners. The remainder were engrossed in conversations aided by pints of ale. Two tossed darts. A few ate dinners of the specialties, fish and chips, and shepherd's pie. A pungent aroma of fried fish, mingled with the ever-present smell of roast beef, permeated the room. Not unpleasant smells. He was satisfied that no one took notice of them. He felt they would not be overheard.

Darnell asked Sheinhofer, "I'm curious. Will you explain why the foreign office would employ a German immigrant such as yourself?"

The man shook his head. "If you think they pass all their secrets by me, sir, you're wrong. I give them information, I don't get any."

"You give them intelligence on Germany? Things that can be useful in the war effort?"

He nodded. "Whatever I can, whatever they need. I know the geography, the major cities, the manufacturing plants. I translate any German documents that fall into their hands."

"Don't they question your loyalties? You're German, aren't you?"

He smiled. "Only half. My father. My mother met him on a trip to Germany. They married there, stayed there, and I was born and grew up there. But we visited England often before the war, and I finally came here when I had to make the choice. I love this country like my own."

"They're not alive, your parents?"

"No. I came here just before the war broke out. My mother wanted to come, but decided to stay with my father. He refused to join the army, said he didn't believe in war. They shot him. I heard from relatives she died a few months later of grief, and I never heard her voice again." He looked down, obviously trying to gain his composure.

Doyle broke in. "You can see why Alfred hates Germany." He looked at Darnell. "He's told me some other things tonight that could be helpful . . . Go ahead, Alfred."

The young man ran a hand through his thinning hair. "It's a disadvantage being half-German and half-English, because neither side quite trusts me. But in another way, it's an advantage, because I've known people on both sides. I knew many of the people at the German Embassy."

"Weren't they all repatriated to Germany when the war started?" Darnell carried on the questioning, studying the man. "The embassy was closed, of course."

"Some managed to stay on here, by hiding out, to do whatever damage they could here as an underground element—sabotage, spying, information-gathering."

"You know where they are?"

"No. I only heard that some stayed."

"Do you have any names?"

"Well, just one. He worked as a handyman and chauffeur at the embassy. Baldrik."

Darnell looked at Doyle. "The name means nothing. What else do you know?"

"They had certain regular visitors at the embassy, mostly at night. Secret visitors, you might say."

"Any names there?"

Sheinhofer nodded. "Haas was one. Of course, I never knew whether the names were real. This one would drink with the second-tier embassy people. He knew a woman there. How do you say, it puffed up his ego. Talking with them, socializing. Maybe more, with her."

"Haas. German. A sympathizer."

"Yes."

"Go on."

"He spoke of places he used to rendezvous with his lady friends. His harlots, more like. He was that type, if you know what I mean."

"And the places? Were they houses? Do you know any addresses?"

"He knew someone of property. He was allowed to

use certain houses that were unoccupied, boarded up. At no cost to him."

"All right, Alfred. Those houses. Where were they?"

"I know of three of them, but only by street name. My friend at the embassy told me Haas would use them whenever he had the whim. Somehow it stuck in my mind." He gave Darnell the street names and their districts.

"You've been a great help."

The young man beamed, and sat back relaxed now, taking large swallows of his beer.

Darnell said to Doyle, "Megan could be at one of these houses. I think this Haas, whoever he is, is involved, and these places could be a connection. We'll have to go to all three."

Doyle raised his eyebrows. "We can't just break into an English home. We need warrants, don't we?"

Darnell said, "I'd consider them *German* homes, if German kidnappers and murderers are there." He paused. "I'll tell O'Reilly about it when I call her. She can get the warrant first thing in the morning. We'll pay these places a visit tomorrow."

Darnell called O'Reilly from a pay phone, gave her the street names and requested the warrants.

Outside the pub, Darnell sat in his car, waiting until Doyle had driven away to drop Sheinhofer off at his place. He checked the street of the first of the three houses on the list, and drove toward it. He would do his own reconnaissance tonight, by himself. Warrants could wait. What Doyle and O'Reilly didn't know wouldn't hurt them.

John Darnell found that the three houses were not widely separated, and were similar as to type—older, large nineteenth-century houses, none of them occupied, most of the windows boarded. The grounds were unkempt, as if no one had lived in any of the homes for months, or even years. They may have housed Germans, Darnell thought, from their embassy or other facilities, and were closed down when the war started two years earlier.

He drove by each home slowly enough to take a good look at it. He knew his car in those quiet neighborhoods might attract attention on a Sunday night, but he found the streets deserted.

The first home had a forbidding if not ghostly aura, and no sign of life. He drove to the second and found that it, too, looked like a place the locals, certainly the children, would claim that ghosts haunted. The third, on a street well beyond the second, appeared too dilapidated, Darnell decided, to be a good hiding place, at least for any long-term purpose.

Darnell drove back to the second home, the one in the best condition, and parked on a small side lane. He decided to reconnoiter, circle around the block and view the back of the house for any lights. He walked down the narrow lane and turned left into a broad street, toward the front of the house down the block. No traffic or pedestrians were out at that hour, understandably so, with light rain in an older, sedate neighborhood. All the residents were home by their fires, he imagined, or even in their beds, at that hour.

He fixed his eyes on the house as he neared it and then passed by, looking straight ahead. He did not slow or stop in front of it, not wanting to be observed. Did he see a flicker of light through a lower window? Was it coming from a basement? He could not be sure. If light had been there, it disappeared quickly. He continued his walk and soon came back around to his car. It was eleven-fifteen.

Darnell waited at the car until almost midnight, considering a last time whether to delay until O'Reilly obtained warrants that morning. Finally, he sighed, said, "Chuck it," and stepped out of the car. He made sure his .38 special and torch were in his pockets, and walked back toward the house. Remembering his experience in the cellar at the medium's house, he knew he'd have to be more careful this time. People were depending on him.

He stayed toward the edge of the walk, along the row of tall trees, to obtain such concealment as he could. He pulled his hat down and turned his collar up against the now-steady light rain. Approaching the bleak, boarded-up home he thought of Megan, and pictured her face in the photograph on Lloyd George's desk. If there was any chance of the girl being there, he knew he had to get inside that house, tonight. Time was running out.

Chapter 20

Darnell crossed the grounds of the house to a row of hedges bordering the walkway to the front door. He crouched behind a hedge, waited, and watched for any display of activity or light in the supposedly deserted house. Minutes passed, then an hour. About to stand up and leave as the time reached one a.m., he was startled by a sliver of light when a side door opened. He held his breath and watched.

Darnell crouched lower, as three men walked out of the doorway. One of them pulled the door shut behind them, and the three continued past Darnell's place of concealment and down the walkway toward a motorcar. He could not see their faces. One grumbled, ". . . thirty minutes isn't much time. Those women better be flamin'." The car started noisily in the quiet night, and they drove off.

When the car was out of sight, Darnell jumped up and ran across the grass to the side door, and was relieved to find that it had a defective latch. He forced the door open, stepped inside, closed it, and looked around the hallway in the dim light to get his bearings. Dust particles filled his air passages.

Darnell clicked on his electric torch and flashed it about the side hall and into empty rooms to his left and right. A stairway in front of him led down to what probably was servants' quarters. A light glowed through a partly opened door, a thin shaft of it streaming across the floor of the hallway.

He pulled out his .38, walked softly down the stairs, and peered through the door into a kitchen. He listened. No sounds at all. It seemed the three who'd left were the only ones there. He pushed the door open and stepped through the doorway quickly.

The kitchen showed signs of use. A coffeepot sat on the stove, and three cups, whiskey bottles, and water glasses on the table. Plates showed a residue of food. Were there prisoners in other rooms? Megan? The medium? He knew he had not much more than a half hour to search the house before they returned.

He began with a quick search of the lower servants' level. His torch revealed splattered red stains on the kitchen floor. "Oh God!" Was it Megan's blood? He shuddered, and stepped around the stains, his throat tight. He worked his way quickly through a bedroom with two small beds and a dresser, the room looking like it had once been occupied by a maid. Now it was strewn with men's clothes. He hurried through two other empty side rooms, and a water closet that showed recent use. But no other signs of life.

Back up the low steps to the main floor, he ran through the main-floor living room, sitting rooms, a library with walls of bare bookshelves, and a glassed-in parlor overlooking the back garden, all the rooms, not surprisingly, without furniture. He found himself at a main staircase opposite the front door. Scuff marks of shoes in the dust showed that someone had entered this way from the front door and gone up the staircase. He ran up the stairs following the light of his torch, narrowly avoiding two broken steps and large cracks in the staircase through which the floor below showed.

The second-floor landing led to a series of bedrooms in either direction. Darnell moved quickly up and down the hall, flashing his light inside every room. At the far end of the hall he found a locked room. He twisted the knob and pushed on the heavy, solid oak door. There was no breaking it. A faint light showed under the door.

Darnell called, "Megan? Who's inside? Can you hear me? I'm a friend."

The voice came eerily through the crack under the door as if from a tomb. "Is it Professor Darnell? It's Madame Ispenska. Help me!"

"Is Megan in there with you?"

"No. I don't know where she is. Get me out of here!"

He pushed against the door harder, but could not move it. "Who's holding you here?"

"Two thugs. Get me out, please!"

Darnell looked about the hall. There was nothing to use as a battering ram, and the door was too strong a barrier. He glanced at his watch. Minutes had passed. He thought quickly. Should he stay, and count on the element of surprise, try to overpower the three men? If he lost that struggle, Megan's safety and even her life could be imperiled. That would be foolhardy. They might never find her. He had to find Megan if she was there.

He called to her, "Is Megan here anywhere? Do you know whether she's in the house?"

"I told you, I haven't seen her. I don't know. Get me out!"

"I can't. They're coming back soon, and I have to look for Megan. I'll be back as soon as I can with the police."

"Don't go!"

"I'll be back. Don't say anything to them."

Come back with reinforcements, his instincts said. That seemed to be the proper course. Also, he felt Lloyd George would think only of his daughter's safety. But he had to finish searching the house in the time remaining.

Darnell ran up the stairs to the third floor, and up and down the halls. More bedrooms, another sitting room and small library, a narrow servants' staircase

leading down to the back of the house. And another
door, as solid as the one to the room the medium was
locked in, seemed to lead up to an attic. He tried it.
It was locked, and he could not budge it. Nor could
he hear any sound on the other side of it. But noises
came from outside, the sound of a car.

Thirty minutes after they left the house, the man
called Haas dropped Baldrik and Slade at its front
walkway. "I'll be back tonight. Just one more day
then."

"You should stay in this rat-trap spiders' home for
jus' one night," Slade said, his words slurred from
drink. "Jus' so you'd know what the bugger hell we
go through here."

"You're drunk, or I'd give you a little hell to consider yourself. You get paid for it. You'll split Karl's
share, don't forget. But only if you take good care of
your guests."

Baldrik said, "Oh, we'll take care of them. Maybe
give 'em a spot of entertainment. The girls might not
half mind it." He enjoyed sticking that needle into the
other man, although after the heavy drinking his
words were not as sharp-edged as usual. "Those street
floosies you got for us tonight weren't exactly beauties,
y'know. What'd they cost you, two shillings for the
lot?"

Haas slammed the car door. "I know you'd be more
keen for a posh hotel. You'd like silk knickers. Beauties. Sure you would. But you'll take what you get, and
like it. Now earn your keep." Haas turned his car
around and drove away.

The two stood side by side watching the car fade
out of view in the night. Baldrik looked at Slade.
"One day he'll get something he don't expect. And
we'll see how he likes it."

"But not until after we're paid," Slade said.

"C'mon, mate. I think there's a half bottle of whiskey left inside. I could use another spot . . . or two."

They stumbled through the side door and tromped

unsteadily down the steps to the kitchen. Baldrik poured two inches of whiskey in glasses, grinned crookedly, and handed one to Slade. " 'Ere's to you, matey."

Darnell heard the sounds of the two men from below, doors opening and closing, footsteps entering the house on the first floor. The men had returned too soon. Damn! Fortunately, they were probably going down into their kitchen area, not upstairs. He had to get out, and through to Scotland Yard. This couldn't wait until morning.

He moved down the servants' staircase on the balls of his feet, softly, as fast as he could without making noise they could hear, without stumbling, down to second floor, then to the first. At last he found himself standing by a back door in a rear hall. Darnell left through the door, opening and closing it as quietly as he could, and, once on the lawn, he ran across it and down to his car. He had to find a phone, and fast.

Baldrik and Slade guzzled half their drinks and collapsed onto the kitchen chairs at the table. Slade whistled a dance-hall tune off-key and tipped his chair back and forth with his foot against the table's edge. Baldrik drank the rest of his whiskey in silence, and refilled his glass. He stared at Slade with a smile playing about the edges of his thick lips.

"I'll check the girl," Slade said. "You do the psychic."

"Hah!" Baldrik's burst of laughter startled the other. "Not bloody damn likely. You'd rape the poor thing, drunk as you are. Besides, she's mine, when this's over."

"What difference would one more, you know, make to a girl?"

"You said it yourself. Did you forget already? *'After we're paid!'* No, it's hands off her for you. I'll look in on the girl. You check on the swami."

Ten minutes later, after finishing their drinks, the

two staggered upstairs, each with an electric torch. Slade walked down the second-floor hall toward the room where the medium was kept. Baldrik continued to the third floor, unlocked the door, and stomped up the attic stairs to the room where Megan was held. He unlocked the second door at the top of the stairs and looked in. She seemed to be asleep. He relocked the door and returned to the second floor. As he reached the landing, he met Slade coming down the hall toward him from the medium's room.

"That crazy woman's acting balmier than ever," Slade said. "She's babbling, *'You're going to get what's coming to you.'* Sounds like a warning. I think she's heard somethin'."

"How could she hear anything up here?"

"I don't know . . . maybe . . . ," he rubbed his head, "while we were gone."

Baldrik scratched his chin, heavy with the long day's beard. "Huh . . . well, let's see her."

They walked back to her room, Slade unlocked it, and they stepped inside. Baldrik walked over to the bedside where Madame Ispenska lay. He removed the sharp-bladed knife he carried at all times in the scabbard of his belt, and tapped her arm with the point of it. "You know somethin' we don't know, dearie?" He considered the point. "Was someone here while we were gone?"

She pulled her arm away. "No. Get out of here so I can sleep."

"Oh, you can sleep, all right. Maybe a long, long sleep." He grabbed her throat with one hand and with the other scraped the reverse side of the knife blade harshly against her cheek. "Do you want to tell us who it was, now, or shall I . . ."

She choked out, "Please. I-I don't know anything. I just told Slade you'll get punished. I meant, by the law."

"Really? Now, why do I think you're lying through your teeth?"

He slapped her across the face with back of his

hand, then again, harder, on the other cheek, her head knocked first in one direction, then the other. "Who was here!" He grabbed her by her long hair and pulled it, twisting it up in one hand.

Tears came to her eyes. "No one! I don't know anything."

Baldrik pushed her down on the bed. He turned and walked out the door. "All right, but we're not through with you . . . Let's get the hell out of here, Slade."

Slade shook his head and followed Baldrik out of the room. "She's a tough gypsy. That bit about the law, about us getting punished. She was just bluffing, eh? Pullin' her crystal ball stuff."

Baldrik locked the door and stood in the hall, frowning, his torch dispelling very little of the gloom in the dark corridor. He rubbed his chin. "No, someone was here while we were away. Let's find a phone booth."

After phoning Scotland Yard and finally reaching Chief Inspector Howard, Darnell again pulled in to the curb where he had parked before. In half an hour Inspector Howard, Sergeant O'Reilly, and four uniformed policemen arrived. O'Reilly had obtained warrants from a midnight judge, and arranged that all officers were armed. Three a.m., and the street and neighborhood were dark and quiet.

"I saw three of them, and they generally stay in the kitchen downstairs," Darnell said, as they stood by his car, "but one may have left. They use the former servants' quarters. The medium is on the second floor, locked in a room. I searched the whole house. The only place Megan could be is in the attic. I had to leave when they returned."

"Then we'll break in and hit that lower floor first," Chief Inspector Howard said.

"Right. But we'll make a hell of a noise breaking in that side door, if they locked it, and I expect they did. Three men should break it in, then stand clear while the rest run down the stairs to the kitchen. They seem to sleep in a side room. Now, they came back to the house late last night. And if they drank a lot . . ."

". . . they'll be slow to respond," O'Reilly said. "We'll have a chance to take them by surprise."

"Let's hope so, because they'll hear us break in."

"Shoot on sight," Howard said. He looked at his men.

"Wait," Darnell said. "If we kill all of them, and Megan isn't here after all . . ."

"You mean, we couldn't question them?" Howard's face was grim. "But what choice do we have? We have to take them. We'll do what we must. If one is alive and can talk, that will help." To his men, he said, "Shoot low. Don't shoot to kill."

"They have the medium here. It's logical that Megan's in this house, too," Darnell said. "So let's go. Just be quiet outside until we break in the door. The less warning they have, the better."

They walked to the house in a ragged line, two wide, then across the grass to the side door. Darnell and O'Reilly led the way, but at the door they stood aside, allowing three bulky uniformed policemen to charge forward and crash through the side door.

Two of the men stumbled with the force of the effort and fell to the floor. Darnell rushed down the stairs, O'Reilly close at his side, both with guns drawn, a uniformed officer behind them with Howard. They burst through the open doorway of the dark kitchen and ran forward into the small maids' bedroom. The room was empty.

Chapter 21

"Damn!" Darnell stared at the two empty beds. "They've flown!"

Howard and O'Reilly stared at him.

"I'm afraid they took Megan." He grabbed the arm of an officer, saying, "Come with me," and ran toward the second-floor stairs.

Chief Inspector Howard said, "I'll search this floor, Sergeant. You look upstairs with Darnell."

Torches shone through the dark rooms as they all moved quickly through the house. O'Reilly and two of the men ran upstairs at Darnell's heels.

Darnell ran to the room where the medium had been imprisoned, but as he arrived saw, with a sinking feeling, that the door was open. She, too, was gone. Her clothes were scattered about on the bed and floor, showing a hurried retreat.

"Megan must be upstairs," he said. "There was a door . . . ." He ran up to the third floor and the door that seemed to lead to an attic. It stood open, and at the top of the stairs, he found a small room with a bed and an adjacent water closet. Obviously Megan's prison. Sergeant O'Reilly stood at his side as he stared at the empty room.

Darnell hit the wall with a fist. "I let them slip through my fingers!"

*   *   *

In the bedroom of their new place of hiding, Slade set his electric torch on a dresser, the spike of light from it creating elongated shadows on the wall. "This dump is worse'n the first one," he said. "You'd almost expect Jack the Ripper to step out of the shadows."

He dumped Megan onto the dusty, bare mattress on the floor as if she were a bundle of rags. Megan groaned, and looked up at him, her eyes filled with tears, and then away.

At the other side of the room Baldrik pushed Madame Ispenska down on the floor with a twisted smile. "Don't wander off."

Madame Ispenska's glare followed him with unconcealed hatred. She glanced at Megan, but the girl's eyes were covered by her arm.

Baldrik scowled as he looked about, and turned to Slade. "You're right. This place is no bloody Taj Mahal." He laughed at his own words, a sharp "Hah!" followed by a peal of his usual bellowing laughter that seemed to shake the glass in the windows.

Slade stared at him, angry at the noise, yet fearful of the other's unpredictable moods. "Hold it down," he snapped, then thought better of it. In a defensive tone, he added in a softer voice, "People are still sleepin' in this neighborhood. You want the police to show up?"

"Relax, matey. There's no neighbors on either side of us. No one to hear us except maybe a few ghosts." He grinned. "And we'll only be here one night. It's almost over now. Then tomorrow, well, that's our payday, and our fun day." He looked over at the girl on the bed.

"We get paid. That's the main thing." Slade glared. "We need to get it from Haas when he shows. I don't trust that bugger."

Baldrik fingered the knife in his belt scabbard. "When I called him, he said he'd be here in a couple of hours. Don't worry, I'll take care of that pantywaist if there's any trouble. Now, let's tie up our guests again, and grab some shut-eye."

Darnell ran a hand through his hair and leaned against the wall of the room where Megan had been held. His forehead was deeply furrowed. He rubbed the knuckles of one hand with the other. "It's my fault. I should have tried to break in here last night and fought it out with the three men."

O'Reilly rested a hand on his arm. "Don't blame yourself, John. You couldn't match three of them. You'd be dead, and we'd never find Megan."

"I've got to think," he said.

They returned to the second floor and Darnell paced up and down in the hallway, waiting for the others.

Inspector Howard and the other officers ran up. "Nothing," Howard said. "Looks like we've lost them."

Darnell scowled.

Still breathing heavily, Howard came up to Darnell. "What is it, John?"

Darnell paced across the room again and back, then stopped. "Megan was here, but they took her away. I let them get away."

Howard said, "Damn. Now what?"

Darnell said, "There's one chance. The other two houses Sheinhofer told us about. No one else knows we're aware they exist. They could have taken Megan and Ispenska to one of them."

"That's it, then, it's our only chance," Howard said, his voice crisp. "We'll split into two teams and hit both houses at once. You and O'Reilly take two officers with you to one house, John. I'll take two men with me to the other place."

Darnell gave directions to both houses to the Chief Inspector. "We'll both probably have to break in. The one you're going to is closer. If they're not there, come on to the third house. We'll be there by then."

Howard said, "Good."

Darnell turned, saying, "Let's go, then. No time to lose. Come on, Sergeant." He ran down the hallway to the stairs, the others following. Within minutes their cars were speeding away.

Darnell pulled up on the side street, a half block from the house, to preserve as much of the element of surprise as possible. He led O'Reilly and the two officers up the street and across the lawn to the deserted, run-down house. He scouted around to the back of it, looking for a way in. When he tried the French doors leading to a parlor, he found to his surprise that they were not locked, although stuck from years of disuse. He pushed the doors open with some effort, but grimaced when they creaked.

His .38 ready, he crossed the room quickly in the dim twilight that filtered through the windows, preceding daybreak. The others followed, also with their weapons out. "Be careful," he whispered to O'Reilly. "They may have heard us."

As they reached the base of a curving staircase leading to the second floor, gunfire flashed from above. The first shot struck the arm of one of the uniformed officers, who dropped to the floor with a groan but was able to pick up his service revolver in the other hand. O'Reilly whirled and fired at the two men on the second-floor landing. One of the men shouted to the other, "Get down, Slade!"

Darnell ran up the stairs toward them, also firing, with the second officer following him. Their own hail of bullets sprayed the upper landing area, but the two men above them returned their volleys. Darnell heard a cry behind him, and the sound of a body falling. He glanced back, and saw blood forming a circular stain on the man's pant leg.

The second man on the landing yelled, "Look out, Baldrik!" Darnell's shots took down his partner, a swarthy sailor type, with two shots, one creasing his head, another apparently lodging in the shoulder. The man hit the floor hard, his gun scattering across it, and he was clearly unconscious when he landed.

Darnell concentrated his fire now on the second man, who threw his empty revolver at Darnell as he reached the landing. Seeing that the man's gun was empty, Darnell charged at him, intent on taking him alive for questioning.

But the young hoodlum fixed his eyes on Darnell with a malevolent glare and pulled a glistening blade from a leg scabbard. Darnell continued his rush toward him, and the two men grappled, falling heavily to the floor. Darnell grabbed the man's hand holding the knife. The man pulled away, his back now to the landing railing. Darnell rushed forward again and hit him full on the chest with his body.

The man struck out with his long-bladed, razor-sharp knife and slashed Darnell's arm, but at the same time the railing behind the man cracked, and he fell through it to the floor below, twisting in the air, with a loud cry of fear and hatred. Darnell grabbed a post of the railing that was still standing and caught himself precariously on the ledge.

He took a breath, pulled back to greater safety, and surveyed the carnage. An officer on the staircase sat holding his leg. A second officer sat on the main floor below, gripping an arm dripping blood with his other hand.

Sergeant O'Reilly lay without moving.

Darnell drew his breath with a sharp intake. Sergeant O'Reilly's face lay in his direction, and her eyes were closed. A small pool of blood had seeped onto the floor around her head.

The man who fell through the balcony railing lay facedown, the tip of his knife blade showing through his back. He had fallen on his own weapon. Darnell checked the man on the landing, the one apparently called Baldrik, who was bleeding from two wounds and was unconscious. He recalled that the name was one Sheinhofer had mentioned in the pub.

Darnell quickly picked himself up, retrieved his gun,

and rushed down the stairs, anxious over the condition of Sergeant O'Reilly. He bent down and checked her pulse. Still beating. "Sergeant! Catherine!" he urged. In response, her eyes still closed, she groaned.

Howard and the two other officers burst into the room from the rear of the house. "My God!" Howard shouted, and stopped short as he took in scene. He looked down at O'Reilly. "Is she . . . ?"

"No, thank God," Darnell said. "She's been unconscious. The bullet caught the side of her head. We have to get her to a hospital, also the officers. One officer has a leg wound, the other took a bullet in an arm. One of the hoodlums upstairs is still alive, but unconscious. I shot him twice."

"We'll call for an ambulance and leave a man here. But we'll take Sergeant O'Reilly and the officers in our car. It's faster." Howard gave orders. His men picked O'Reilly up and carried her to a car, then helped the injured officers.

Howard looked down at the dead man who had fallen on his own knife. "Who are these men?"

Darnell shook his head. "All we know now is that they kidnapped Megan. They look like hired thugs. The one upstairs is only wounded and should live, might talk. I heard the other call his name—Baldrik. Sheinhofer mentioned his name tonight, called him a former German Embassy employee." He gestured at the dead man. "Both of them used their knives as if they enjoy carving up people . . . Oh God, knives. These must be the same thugs who attacked Penny."

"A fit way for this one to die," Doyle said.

Darnell stood, holding his bleeding arm with the other hand. "I'm wasting time. Megan. I've got to search the house for Megan." He ran to the stairs.

"Can you manage?" Howard asked, running beside him. "Your sleeve's soaked with blood."

"It can wait." Darnell took the stairs two at a time and ran up and down the second-floor hallway. Howard followed. The door of one room stood open and

Darnell found Madame Ispenska inside, bound and gagged. Her wide eyes begged for help.

He pulled the gag from her mouth. "Are you all right . . . Is Megan here?"

The medium coughed and breathed in sharply, choking. "I'm all right. The girl was here but Stanton took her away with him."

"Stanton? Hugo Stanton? He was the one?" Darnell said, and he and Howard looked at each other.

"My God," Howard said.

"When did he leave?"

"A half hour ago."

"Damn! We're always one step behind him. What can you tell me? I have to find her."

She shook her head as if to clear it, or remember. "I overheard Stanton talking to one of them. But they called him Haas. That was his mother's maiden name, I remember Hugo telling me that."

Darnell untied the medium's hands and feet, and she rubbed them briskly.

"Quick then," Darnell urged, "what do you remember?"

She coughed again. "The girl was gagged, but kicking and trying to hit the one called Baldrik. When Stanton took her away, he said some words to Baldrik, and smiled. An evil smile!" She shuddered. "He said, *'I'm going to the country. Two hostages are better than one.'*" She rubbed her arms where ropes had bound her.

Darnell leaned against the wall, his eyes showing the new fear that suddenly flooded his being. The words echoed in the mind, "*. . . to the country . . . two hostages . . .*"

Howard said, "We're leaving for the hospital now. The ambulance will be here for the two criminals soon." About to leave, he stared at Darnell, whose face seemed drained of blood. "Did you hear me, John . . . What's wrong?"

Darnell spoke his next words in a flat, dead voice, as much to himself as to the Inspector. "Stanton has

Megan—and I'm sure he's gone to our Cotswolds place. To take Penny hostage."

The cars sped away again, the police with the wounded thug, the officers, and Sergeant O'Reilly. Darnell drove in a different direction, toward a train station. His mind flooded with thoughts. He suspected that Stanton had found out he'd sent Penny to their country home in the Cotswolds for safety. Other men must have been following them to the station when he put her aboard the train.

He knew Stanton couldn't take Megan as a prisoner on a train to the Cotswolds, and would have to drive. So there was a faster way to his Cotswolds home. The train. If his timing and the train's schedule were right, he could beat Stanton to his home. He knew a train left for that area at seven A.M. He pushed his car to the limit.

After anxious minutes, Darnell reached the station, rushed in, bought his ticket, and placed a call to Penny at his country home. The connection seemed to take forever, and when the operator tried to ring the number there was no answer. The usual problem with home phone lines in the country. Just when you needed it, he fumed, your phone didn't work. But he knew Stanton couldn't have arrived there yet.

Darnell called Scotland Yard next and, finding Inspector Howard out, left a message for the Inspector to have the local constable in the Cotswolds go to his home to be sure Penny was all right. Then he called his caretaker, asking him to pick him up at the train station nearest his home by Stow-on-the-Wold.

As the train slowly chugged out of the station, Darnell ran alongside it, pulled open his compartment door, jumped inside, and snapped the door shut. The train continued its slow curving exit from the station.

Collapsing onto the seat, Darnell saw that his left sleeve was now soaking wet with blood. He opened the corridor door, looking for a conductor. He put his head out and called to one who was taking a ticket several doors down. When the man reached him, he handed him a pound note. "Bring some bandages, soap and water. I've had a bit of an accident."

The conductor stared at Darnell's arm for a moment, said, "Right away, Guv'nor," turned abruptly, and ran down the corridor.

Darnell exhaled breath he'd been holding. The conductor returned soon with bandages and iodine and dressed Darnell's wound. The cut had not reached the bone and, fortunately, was on the left arm.

After the conductor left, Darnell leaned back in the seat and thought of Penny. He'd been foolish to send her north, out of his sight. But if all went well now, he could reach his home before Stanton and wait there for him. Then his greatest challenge in the case would come when Stanton arrived, the chance to capture him and release the Prime Minister's daughter. He had to be up to it.

Chapter 22

Monday morning, December 18, 1916

After a night of little sleep in their Cotswolds home, Penny was relieved when the local constable came to her door at seven a.m.

"Russell Kinney, ma'am. Inspector Howard just called and asked me to look in on you. I, ah, don't know all the reasons. Your husband was worried."

"Worried? But . . ."

"Husbands do worry, ma'am."

She frowned. "So. Your phone works?"

The constable nodded. "The lines are up now in my area. But we've had a lot of trouble with them lately. The call came through not more than half an hour ago. I came right over." He stepped in, crossed the room to her phone, and lifted the receiver off the hook. "Yours is still dead. But it should work soon."

"Well, anyway, I'm all right. Thanks for coming by. I guess you can leave then."

Constable Kinney stood shifting his weight from one foot to the other. "I, ah, was asked to stay with you, just until your husband arrived."

The words startled her. "John's coming up here? What's happening? I don't understand."

Kinney shook his head. "I've been told he'll be here in an hour or two. He's on the train, heading north."

Penny fought the feelings of helplessness and frus-

tration growing in her mind. An hour or two. She'd
have to wait. She had no choice. At least she knew
he was alive and would be with her soon. She heaved
a sigh. "Some coffee, then, Constable? Shall I make
some?"

She was pleased the constable said yes. It would
give her something to do until John came. She stared
out the kitchen window at the bleak morning. She'd
gotten through the night after their caretaker, Pardlow, had driven her to their home. And she was safe
from the thugs who had threatened her, so John
needn't worry about her. But now she worried about
him.

David Lloyd George felt he had been lying to his
wife for two days, saying he'd do anything to save
Megan. Actually, he had no idea at all what he could
do or would do the following day when he must speak
at the Commons. He'd blocked that from his mind.
He and Margaret sat and poked at their food at the
breakfast table, eating little, at least drinking coffee,
but looking more haggard than their years, much older
in the past four long days.

"Tomorrow's your speech, Davy," she said. It was
the first time he could recall her calling him Davy, her
affectionate term for him, since, well, since before that
first affair he'd had, years ago. After that fierce burning night of argument when she found out about the
woman, he knew she had resigned herself to his infi-
delities, and had settled into the life of a patient politi-
cian's wife, keeping an image for the public. He had
guilt about it, but knew his own failings.

After that, however, she always called him, more
formally, David. And he knew she was letting him
know by that it was never to be as it once was between
them. They now had an understanding that their life
was something far short of the initial flurry and flush
of married love.

Lloyd George nodded. "I may have to say things I
don't intend to enforce, in order to get Megan back.

I'll say anything, do anything for that dear little girl.
I could endorse the peace proposals, then go back on
them afterward. It would be the end for me, when it
came out, but we'd have her back."

She nodded with unusual spirit. "Yes, you can revoke what you say. You have that power." She looked
at him as if for reassurance her words were true.

"Yes. But a Prime Minister with that reputation, a
man forced to lie, a man going back on his word . . .
I'd lose their confidence. I'd be the shortest-lived
Prime Minister in England's glorious history. They'd
throw me out, bag and baggage."

"The people would understand, when they knew
the reasons."

"Don't worry then. You know I'll do it, if need be.
I'm just saying you should be prepared, dear. You
might not be a Prime Minister's wife for much
longer."

"I don't care. I never really cared at all. It was
always for you, for what you wanted." She dried her
tears. "All I want is my little girl. Bring her back to
me, Davy. Bring her back."

He patted her hand. They had to get Megan back.
And then, he wondered, would he and Maggie be
drawn closer by all of this?

Suddenly she put both hands over her mouth. "Oh,
Davy, I just realized something. In one week it will
be Christmas! And our baby is still in some kind of
terrible prison."

"It will be all right. She'll be with us on Christmas.
I swear it." But he knew his very words were equal
to another lie. He could guarantee nothing. As Prime
Minister, Lloyd George knew he was the most powerful man in England, yet in this matter he was power-
less and could achieve his daughter's release not by
showing his strength, but by yielding it. By surren-
dering.

Lloyd George had decided he could not force himself to go to the War Cabinet room again, so instead

he asked the members to come to Downing Street for the last, early morning meeting before the reconvening of the Commons the next day.

They met in the conference room adjacent to his office after he left the breakfast room following his final reassurances to Maggie.

They had come promptly, even at the early hour, and that pleased Lloyd George.

The Prime Minister studied his cabinet. Bonar Law, his right hand, evoked a power of his own in his stable, advisory way. Lloyd George felt Law could be a worthy successor, if he himself were forced out over this affair. Adler, Curzon, Milner, Henderson, and Addison, experts in their own fields, were all vital members of the cabinet.

To Lloyd George, it seemed days since their last meeting, so much had happened. "I called you together, my friends, to let you know where I stand, for tomorrow's Commons meeting. We have not recovered my daughter."

Groans and expressions of condolences greeted his words. Bonar Law asked, "Nothing from Scotland Yard?"

"They came close to finding her, even last night, and this morning. But the criminal slipped through their fingers. We may know more today."

"What will you do?"

"What will I do? Exactly. That's the question, and that's why you're here." He stood and paced back and forth across the width of the conference room, then stopped and faced the group. "I think I have several options, but they are all extremely confidential, and I expect all of you to respect that."

"Of course," Law said. "I'm sure I speak for all of us."

The others nodded, murmured assent.

"First choice, if Megan is not recovered in time, before I must speak, I will lie to the Germans. I'll say I will endorse the peace proposals. Then when I have Megan back, I will revoke my position."

Curzon said, "That's dangerous. Those who want to end the war would move fast to consolidate that victory."

"Second choice, I resign as Prime Minister, hoping they would release Megan, knowing they'd have no leverage over me anymore."

"Would they do that? Release her?" Curzon's voice showed his concern.

"It would be a gamble. Along those lines, I've thought of a third alternative. They might release her, knowing their leverage was gone, and deliberations on the peace proposals could be delayed—if I were not alive."

Bonar Law jumped up and stared at the Prime Minister. "My God, David! What are you saying?"

Lloyd George waved his hands. "Sit down, Bonar. Don't take my words literally. It would be a subterfuge, a news report of my death, from an assassin's bullet. But I'd be in hiding, out of sight. Hopefully, you, Bonar, would take over the government and pull our forces together. Then after Megan was safe, I could turn up again, perhaps just as an MP."

The room was silent. Law said, finally, "You know that none of those choices are acceptable, David. But we'll follow your lead tomorrow. Do whatever you have to do. We'll support you."

Adler and Milner, together, said, "Hear, hear."

Lloyd George nodded. It had all come down to that. He would do what he had to do.

Chapter 23

Monday morning, December 18, 1916

John Darnell, never a man given to nervousness, found himself checking the time over and over throughout the morning as the train traveled in its northwesterly course toward the station nearest Stow-on-the-Wold, the area in which his country home was located. He flexed his left arm, which the conductor had bandaged, and tested it. It ached, but he could use it if he were careful.

He clicked open the lid of his pocket watch and looked at the time again. Seven-thirty a.m. He ran a hand through his hair. The train would reach the station in a half hour, and he guessed it would take a half hour more to reach his place from there by car. That should put him home before nine a.m. But how much of a head start did Stanton have? Could Stanton arrive before the train?

Darnell stared out of the window. Penny's face seemed to appear before his eyes in the sooted, mirrorlike glass. And the sound of laughter of a woman walking by in the corridor reminded him of his wife. He frowned, and drummed his fingers on the edge of the window. Couldn't this blasted train go any faster?

Hugo Stanton pulled his car to the side of the road and cut the engine. For the third time in the past half hour he swore as he picked up his map. The confusing array of main roads and side roads depicting the country northwest of London had lost him at least an hour as he searched for the correct route. He mumbled under his breath, "How can anyone find his way around here?"

After leaving the second house with Megan gagged and tied up in the backseat, he had driven about London fuming, thinking of Darnell's interference. He was determined to take Penny Darnell as a second hostage. Maybe then Darnell would stop meddling. He had found the flat of the man who had followed her to the Darnell country home area and reported back to Stanton by phone. Through a secluded back entrance, he took Megan in and deposited her on a bed. He faced his man as he looked at scribbles on a single sheet of paper the man handed him.

He glared at him. "Are these all the notes you took on directions? How am I supposed to find that damn place?"

"Sorry, must've been under the weather a bit."

Stanton grunted. "Hah! Your pint of whiskey on the train."

The other did his best to describe stores and pubs along the way and landmarks, such as a square-towered church, apparently famous in the area, but his information was garbled. Stanton stayed at the small house long enough to go over the notes, eat, give food to the girl, and sleep for as long as he dared. He had lost valuable time. But directions or not, he knew he had no choice. He left in a foul mood and began the long drive north.

Now, after driving for three hours, he found himself without food, with only drinking water in the car, and heading up another wrong-turn road. Realizing he'd have to double back again, his temper rose. And the occasional moans of his hostage on the floor of the backseat did nothing to improve his mood. At least, he thought, the girl didn't talk constantly. His threat to put a gag back on her seemed to have worked.

He glanced back at the bound girl, but immediately regretted looking at her when her moist, soulful eyes bored into his.

"Can't you take these ropes off?" Megan pleaded. "My arms and legs are hurting. I can't run away."

"When we stop next," he said. "I'll loosen them then."

During the long drive. Stanton engaged in the periodic soul-searching his mixed heritage had made part of his nature. He thought back to the first talks of war, when his mother had urged him to assist the pacifists. It seemed a fitting revenge for his treatment as a half-German in England. Schoolmates had called him "Hun." And his mother suffered worse names.

Later, native Britishers at government offices where he worked looked askance at his German background after the war broke out. Not—he thought now, with a twisted smile—without some justification.

The death of Brent had resulted from the orders of others, he had rationalized at the time, but now that it was all over, he regretted the man's death. And since he had taken personal charge of the child now, he found the plot to kidnap her—which had once seemed something distant for him, a matter of merely giving orders to others, not something he had to deal with personally—more excruciating than he'd expected. He was forced to see her misery here, in his own car, to hear her voice and look into her eyes. Worst of all, Megan reminded him, with a renewed sadness, of his sister of twelve, Gerthe, who had died of influenza a year earlier. Stanton could not avoid comparing his memories of his own sister to the girl in his car. With two years' more life, she'd have been Megan's age.

Conflicting thoughts fogged Stanton's mind. He thought of turning back to London. But when he imagined the emotional outburst he could expect from his mother, and the need to face the anger of those who had given him his distasteful orders, he steeled himself to continue. He swore aloud, "Damn the mapmakers! Damn these roads! Damn it all!"

He had lost time, and suspected the police and the meddling professor had discovered the last hiding place by now. Would they get onto his plan? Or could he steal up here and do what he needed to do without interference?

Stanton gritted his teeth and pushed the conflicting feelings from his mind. He must concentrate on his goal, and reach the professor's house before they stumbled on what he was doing.

Words from the backseat broke through his thoughts. "Can't we stop? I'm hungry. And, and . . . these ropes hurt."

He looked at the girl again and, with a sigh, said, "All right."

He stopped the car and reached back to loosen the ropes from her hands and feet. The sight of the red marks on her arms and legs bothered him.

"We'll leave them off for a while," he said, then warned, "but any problems, the ropes go back on."

Megan took a deep breath through her mouth. "I promise," she said, her voice hoarse.

Stanton unscrewed the top of a container and turned to her. "Water?" When she nodded, he handed her the container.

Megan looked at his face, as she took several large gulps, but he avoided her gaze. She said, "Th-thank you."

Stanton jerked his attention back to his map. After a moment, in exasperation, he tossed it aside and started the car. He swung around, drove back to the last side road, and turned into it, heading in what he hoped was the right direction.

Running late, at eight-thirty A.M., the London train chugged into the station nearest Stow-on-the-Wold and John Darnell jumped off before it stopped moving. He was relieved to see the caretaker for his home waiting on the platform. Wade Pardlow looked after several houses, including Darnell's, to supplement his income from running a local grocery store. With Darnell's infrequent visits to the country, he relied on Pardlow to handle local matters.

The man, dressed in country tweeds and a brimmed brown cap, strolled over to him on the platform in his typical relaxed style. He looked around and asked, "No bags, sir?"

Darnell said, "No. Mrs. Darnell is at the house?"

"Yes, sir. Took her there last night, as you instructed."

Darnell strode to the telephone box. The operator rang his home several times, but the line was dead.

"Let's go, Wade. And make it fast." Darnell looked at the vehicle, little more than a jalopy, parked at the edge of the station. "Is that your car?"

"Yes, sir."

Darnell hoped he could make Pardlow aware of the urgency, without revealing the entire story. He made long strides toward the car. Pardlow took quick steps to keep up with Darnell. "You're in a hurry, sir."

"Indeed. I must get home soon."

Two minutes later they had turned onto the two-lane road that led toward the village where Darnell's house was located. Pardlow drove competently, but not as fast as Darnell wanted. He itched to get his own hands on the wheel. "All right, there are no bobbies about, Wade," he prodded in an edgy voice. "Give it some more petrol."

"Doing my best, sir, but this car . . ." The car's speed increased only slightly.

Darnell said, "Floor it." He gritted his teeth and looked out of the window in exasperation.

They were now passing familiar landmarks. With his mind on Penny and Stanton, the great beauty of the Cotswolds that had first attracted him to the area only impinged vaguely now on his subconscious. They skimmed by quaint villages with thatched-roof cottages formed with the native limestone as part of their walls. Groves of silvery gray, smooth-barked beech trees stood on the horizon.

Fields bordered by moss-covered, honey-colored stone fences. Wide pastures, serving as home for placid sheep cropping the green grass. Sparkling trout streams that appeared here and there and wound their way through the greenery. Gently rolling hills bristling with stands of oak and elm.

The narrow country lane that they followed now twisted its way through the surrounding fields. In the distance Darnell saw the familiar square towers of a church he'd seen on previous trips. But the beauty of the picturesque land did not seep into his thoughts, and it did nothing to calm his fears. His mind was filled with visions of Penny, as he tried to persuade himself that he'd find she was all right.

At last Darnell exhaled a deep breath he had been holding, and snapped back to reality. The thought came that Stanton could somehow be at the house already. "Faster, Wade. For God's sake!"

The caretaker gave him a gap-toothed grin. "Any faster, and the bloomin' rubber would fly off the wheels." But he pressed the accelerator of the old car to the floor. Darnell could see they were at the best speed he could expect from it, and heard the rattling of metal, something loose somewhere underneath, but he clenched his teeth and fists in his tension.

He realized he couldn't tell Pardlow all the circumstances. He knew Pardlow's relaxed nature, and how he'd react if told a murderer could be waiting for them at his home. Pardlow would turn the car around and head back to the station.

Five minutes later the caretaker drove up the dirt drive to the front of the two-story brick cottage with small-paned windows and topped with a dark blue thatched roof. An acre immediately surrounding the property was bordered by thick green hedgerows and walls of the local rock and stones.

Darnell eyed the second car that sat in front of the house. It could be the constable's. He jumped out of

Pardlow's car as it rolled to a stop, saying, "Thank you, Wade. I'll call you if I need you."

The caretaker nodded and drove off.

As Darnell reached the door, the local constable pulled it open for him and stood with Penny behind him. Darnell ran past the officer and swept her into his arms. "Thank God! You're all right." He hugged her roughly.

Penny's eyes asked questions. "You've really had me worried, John . . . phone calls to the police, the constable coming here. What's it all about?"

"It's all right now."

He turned to the young constable. "Thank you, Russell."

"My duty, sir. And pleasure."

Darnell had decided on the train he could not expose the newly married constable to the danger of that day by keeping him there. He also had to have a safe place for Penny to stay. He'd have to face this challenge alone.

"Are the phones working yet, Russell?"

Constable Kinney nodded. "Yes, sir, just some trouble with the lines, cleared up now."

"I'd like you to take Mrs. Darnell to your place for the day, maybe the night. It will be safer there. Will you?"

He raised his eyebrows. "Why—of course."

"What? John . . . ?" Penny asked, her eyes worried.

"Let's go upstairs, dear. You can pack a few things while I explain."

She found an overnight case as he told her how Stanton had taken Megan with him, and why he expected them to come there. "Just get together what you'll need for a day. But hurry." He paced up and down as she opened dresser drawers.

She tossed a few clothes in the bag. "If he comes, you'll be in danger, John. And if he doesn't, you won't be able to save Megan. I don't know what I want."

He scowled. "I'm convinced he'll be here. If not, well, I'd have to go back to London and search for

Megan. But, if I do go back, I'm sure of one thing. I'm taking you with me. I won't leave you up here alone again."

"Strange, how that man was killed by the very knife they held to my face." She shuddered.

"It was ironic retribution for the thug. Stanton worries me more. In his way, he's more dangerous, a political fanatic."

She took a jacket from a closet, snapped the bag shut, and glanced about the room. "He's a fanatic? You think his German mother taught him hate for England?"

"It could be. But even so, none of that justifies him being a traitor and a murderer."

Penny pulled on the jacket. "Poor Megan. What she must be going through."

"She's got to be with him, otherwise, I don't know . . ." He put his arm around her shoulder. "Are you ready? Let's go."

Darnell walked out to the constable's car with Penny and kissed her in a long embrace. She clung to him for some moments before finally stepping into the front seat.

"Don't worry," he said. "I'll talk with you on the phone. It'll be fine."

He took Kinney aside, a few steps away. "Don't discuss this with Mrs. Darnell, Russell, but the situation here is dangerous. With your help, I won't have to worry about her safety."

Kinney said, "My wife will be with Mrs. Darnell. I'll come back and drive by later, sir, once or twice, to keep an eye on the place. I'll be careful, of course." He shook Darnell's hand and jumped into the car.

The car raised dust. Penny looked back at Darnell and lifted a hand. He watched until the car was out of sight. All that remained was to lie in wait and prepare for Stanton.

Chapter 24

Late in the day, Stanton gave in to the need to stop for food for himself and the girl, selecting a quiet-looking store in a small village. No cars were parked in front of the store. Through the store window, he saw no one but a white-haired man, standing behind the counter.

"I'll buy some food," he said to Megan. He warned, "Don't make any noise. There's no one around to hear you, except me. And I won't like it if I do."

He parked the car where he could watch it every minute through the store window. He retied her legs and arms loosely, and threw a car blanket over her on the floor of the backseat. In the store he made his purchases quickly, keeping an eye on the car. No other customers entered while he was there, and he was soon back in the car and on the road.

A mile away from the store, he pulled off the highway into a woods where they would not be visible from the road. He moved to the backseat, threw the blanket off Megan, propped her up so she could sit against the seat, and removed the rope from her hands and legs.

He put meat slices between his rough cuts of the rustic white bread, and handed her a sandwich. He thrust a small, cold bottle of milk, cap off, into her other hand. She smiled, and began to eat. He wolfed down his own sandwich, made himself another, and drank greedily from a beer bottle.

Megan kept her inquiring eyes fixed disturbingly on him as they ate, and her gaze seemed to bore into his own. When they finished eating, Megan spoke haltingly. "You worked for my father. Do you hate him? Why . . . why are you keeping me like this? Are you going to kill me?" Her lips trembled.

Stanton struggled with his ambiguous feelings at the questions. "You wouldn't understand."

Tears welled in her eyes. "Then it's true. You *are* going to kill me."

"No!" he burst out, unexpectedly, disturbed with himself. "Stop saying that. It's, well, it's a political thing. Nothing to do with you. You wouldn't understand."

"It's the war, isn't it? My father being Prime Minister, and all."

Stanton studied her. "How old are you, then?"

"Fourteen."

"What do you know about wars?"

He reached for another bottle of beer. He was surprised when she answered.

"Men get killed. I know that much."

He looked at her. "Then, should people try to stop wars?"

"I-I suppose."

"That's what I'm trying to do."

"By killing people?" Her eyes stared unwaveringly into his.

"My grandparents . . . they're in Germany. Maybe they'll get killed. I want to stop the war. I have to stop it."

"You're German?"

He nodded. "Half. My mother was born there. My father was English."

"I'm sorry."

Stanton scowled at her words. She was sorry. Yes, so was he. He looked away, feeling his eyes burn. He was angry, too, angry with himself. He threw his empty beer bottle out of the open window.

"Have to get going." He snapped the words out. This vacillation must end, he told himself. *Remember your mission.*

He retied the girl's arms and legs and returned to the front seat. He inspected his revolver and dropped it into his side pocket. Once more he scanned his map and notes, before driving off.

Two miles down the road Stanton's eyes narrowed and his hands gripped the wheel tighter as he saw through the dusk a directional sign set into the dirt border: "Stow-on-the-Wold. Twenty Miles."

After Penny left, Darnell walked through the house checking all the windows and doors to be sure they were locked. He moved a large chair near the front windows where he could watch the road.

He placed a call to Scotland Yard. After a long delay in getting a connection, he heard Chief Inspector Howard's voice come on.

"What's happening there, John?" Howard asked. "Any sign of Stanton?"

"No. I'm getting anxious."

"I'm happy to say Sergeant O'Reilly has been treated, and that she'll recover nicely. The two officers were treated and sent home. The kidnapper's under guard in the hospital with head and shoulder wounds. He'll live, and be tried."

"Any other developments?"

"We've run out of ideas where to search for the girl. If Stanton's not on his way to your place, I just don't know. We'll have to start all over here."

After they rang off, Darnell realized the irony of it. His best and possibly only opportunity to save Megan would be if Stanton brought her to him.

He knew Stanton could come at any time. Twice during the day Darnell saw the constable drive by their home. As the day wore on, Darnell concluded that Stanton was either delayed leaving London, or was waiting until dark. Night fell early in December, and by five p.m., a cloak of darkness had already settled over Stow-on-the-Wold and the surrounding homes. At five-thirty, Darnell called the constable.

"Have you seen anything, Russell? I'm beginning to wonder if he's coming at all."

"No, sir. I've driven by twice and haven't seen a thing. But I'll come by once more."

Darnell spoke to Penny for a few minutes, and was satisfied she was all right. He hung up the phone and sat in the darkened house, no lights at all on now, and focused his attention on the dirt road and the main road beyond. His .38 special lay on the table within easy reach.

Approaching the village, Stanton felt he now had his bearings straight enough to find the Darnell place even in the dark. The girl was an annoyance, squirming about in the backseat. He looked back at her. No gag, and she had not called out, a good sign. Still, he couldn't untie her hands and legs this time. He'd be there in minutes.

"What are you going to do?" she asked.

Stanton made no response. There was no way to answer her, since he questioned his actions himself, although committed to what he saw as a duty. He pulled to the side of the road, offered her water from his container, and watched as she drank from it. He finished what was left of it himself and tossed the bottle away.

"It's time now," he said to himself, under his breath. The country road was bleak and dark, the primary light coming from the full moon. Following the roads carefully, checking his map when light was available from a store window as they passed, he came closer to the road leading to the Darnell home. He saw the home now, through the trees. Before reaching it, he pulled well off the road and parked behind a stand of trees opposite the home. It was pitch dark now, time to act. He grasped his gun in one pocket, a knife in the other, and took a deep breath.

Constable Kinney drove past the Darnell house again, continuing down the road for a mile or so. He turned and drove back past the house. He peered at first one side of the road and then the other, knowing the woods and heavy foliage offered natural hiding places, but he saw no evidence of anything unusual. He continued another mile in the same direction, but saw nothing.

He sighed and said to himself, "One more time." He turned the car around and headed toward the Darnell home. This time he noticed tire tracks leading away from the road, apparently traveling into the woods, or out of it. Had Stanton pulled off, waited there and gone to the Darnell house? Was he still there? He would have to find out.

He drove up the dirt road to the Darnell house. No car was there, a positive sign, but he looked right and left as he walked up to the door and rapped.

Darnell opened it. "Come in. What's happening?"

"Someone's about," Kinney said after he stepped inside. "I saw tire tracks down below, off the road, into the woods."

Darnell's eyes glistened. "Then he's here, somewhere. Listen, Russell, he wants to come to the house. He thinks Penny's here alone. But he won't do it with your car here."

"But, sir . . ."

"You're going to have to leave right away, and let him see you drive off, if he's watching."

"You'll need help."

Darnell's voice was determined. "Leave now, Russell. Just drive away slowly. Go home, and stay there with Penny. I'll feel better if I know you're there with her. I'll call you later on. It's the only way I can confront him. He thinks Penny's here by herself, and doesn't know I'm here. He has to be lured into the trap."

Reluctantly, Constable Kinney left the house and drove down the dirt road. Back on the main road, he slowed down at the juncture where the tire tracks seemed to proceed either into or out of the woods. He studied the marks, hesitant, undecided, remembering Darnell's orders.

Alone on his rounds much of the time, Kinney often voiced his thoughts aloud. "Damn," he said. "What if those tire tracks are going *into* the woods, not *out*. And he's still in there?" He made his decision. As constable, he should investigate. It was a matter of duty.

He cut his car motor and closed the door softly. Not armed, he picked up his nightstick and walked along the tire tracks as they curved through the brush, between the trees. He glanced back, and saw that his car was no longer visible from that angle. When he looked forward again, he made out the dark shape of another car.

Chapter 25

Stanton turned to the backseat and tightened the bindings on Megan's hands and feet, tying one loop to the seat post. "Sorry, little bird, but this has to go on," he said, as he put a gag on her mouth. "And I have to cover you." He tossed the blanket loosely over her and stepped out of the car.

The house was but a few minutes' walk away now. He tipped his hat brim down and his collar up. He gripped his gun tightly in one coat pocket and his knife in the other, and took one last look inside the car.

He was about to walk toward the house when he heard a noise somewhere between the road and where he was standing. He moved quickly behind a tree. Footsteps came his way, but in the dark he could not make out the figure. He held his gun in one hand, but knew he could not shoot, because it would destroy his element of surprise. He pulled the knife from his other pocket.

He watched as a man walked up to the car and peered into its darkness. Stanton rushed behind him and struck at his back with the knife, just as the man turned. The knife missed the man's back, but plunged into his arm, and the man cried out in pain. Stanton struck him with the butt of his gun. He stepped back as the man fell into the underbrush, dropping something he was carrying. Stanton bent down to examine it. A nightstick. The man was a constable. He struck him again on the back of the head with the nightstick and tossed it on the ground.

Megan heard the noises, a man's groan, and the sound of a body falling outside the car. But was it her captor, killed by someone else, or . . . ? She desperately wanted to know.

She waited for some moments, until she heard footsteps moving away from the car and until their sounds faded in the distance. Then she sat up, pushed the blanket off her body, and squirmed over to look out the window.

It was almost pitch black, with only light from the moon filtering down through the thick tree branches, but she could see the outlines of a man's body on the ground. The clothes were different. It was not Stanton. The man was not moving and she thought he might be dead. But she had to get out and see whether she could help him. Then maybe he could help her.

Although her arms and legs were still bound, Megan managed to release the car door handle with her elbow. An owl hooted somewhere in the woods, startling her. She tried to step out of the open door, but with her legs bound together and tied to the seat, she stumbled awkwardly and fell forward onto her outstretched arms. She struck her head on the hard ground, half in the car, half out, and her gag came loose. She was dazed and everything went black. In moments, she stirred and looked again at the man. The moon filtered down onto him now, and she saw it was an officer. He groaned.

"Can you hear me?" she called. "Help me." His eyelids flickered and he pulled himself up to a sitting position. Seeing the girl, he stood, shakily, and moved to her side.

*   *   *

John Darnell stood in the living room looking out the window toward the road. There were no exterior lights, but the full moon afforded enough illumination for him to see the road and any car that would pass or approach the house. He held his .38 special tightly now, and fixed his gaze intently on the road.

He listened, also intently, but heard only an occasional night-bird call. The sound of an owl hooting in the woods oddly reminded him of his years as a boy on the farm in America, when he would lie in bed at night in the room he shared with his brother, Jeffrey, listening to night sounds before falling asleep.

Suddenly his thoughts were broken by the shattering crash of the glass French doors of the sitting room behind him. A man had broken through them. Darnell whirled and faced the man. He heard the words from the other—"My God, it's you!"—and gunshots exploded at him from the direction of the doors.

A bullet chipped wood from the table at his side. He dropped to the floor, tipped over a large cushioned chair, and took a position behind it. He fired back several times in the direction of the doors, but could see only shadows now, not the man.

Two more shots came from that area. One ricocheted off the wooden side of the chair. The shape of a man seemed to move and take cover beside a heavy sideboard against the wall. Darnell waited, instinctively holding his breath, and took careful aim. When he saw what seemed to be a man's body moving again in the dark, he fired at the shape or shadow. There was the groan of a man in pain, the noise of an object resounding through the room as it dropped on the hardwood floor, and then the sound of a man's body hitting the floor.

As Darnell rushed to the man's side, he saw moonlight glinting off the gun on the floor. He kicked the gun away and looked down at the man. Clicking on a table lamp, he saw that his bullet had caught him full in the chest, and the wound was bleeding profusely. The man was Stanton.

"Stanton," he said, bending down low to the man's face.

"Yes." The word gurgled in Stanton's throat. Blood spilled from the corner of his mouth as he spoke. "I-I . . . It wasn't supposed to be this way . . ." He swallowed something in his throat. ". . . wouldn't have hurt your wife." His head jerked to one side.

"Where's the girl, Stanton? Speak up, man."

"She's all right . . . My car, in the woods, not far . . ."

The man's voice weakened with each word. "You're for it, Stanton," Darnell urged. "Who gave you your orders?"

Stanton's eyes were closed. "Little girl . . . I'm sorry, tell her . . ."

"Yes, yes, but who was behind all this?"

". . . victory . . . the key . . ."

"Yes?" Darnell leaned forward, but the man's lips stopped moving and his eyes stared up at the ceiling without seeing it. Darnell shuddered. Watching a man, even a criminal, die before his eyes offered no pleasure. Dying, how could the poor wretch still talk of victory for his cause? A fanatic, and yet . . . He shook his head. Must get to Megan.

He took a deep breath, grabbed an electric torch, and ran through the broken glass of the French doors and across the field toward the woods. In the woods, he tramped through the brush in the dark, in one direction and the other, until he made out the shape of the car.

A man on the ground leaning against the car called, "Over here."

Darnell saw that it was Constable Kinney. Megan sat next to him.

Darnell ran to her and swept her up into his arms. "Thank God! I'm Professor Darnell, I'm working for your father. Are you all right?"

"My arms and legs hurt. Constable took the ropes off." Her voice choked with the words and her eyes filled with tears. She leaned against his shoulder and cried with shuddering, wracking sobs. Darnell felt his own eyes burning.

He rubbed her wrists and ankles vigorously. "Is that better?"

She nodded. Her eyes were still filled with tears. "I want to see my mother and daddy"

Darnell smiled. "I know. And we'll get you there, just as fast as we can. On the train, tomorrow morning. We'll call them on the phone tonight, and you can talk with them. You're safe now."

Carrying Megan in his arms, Darnell stepped over to the Constable's side. "Can you walk, Russell?"

The Constable pushed himself up with his uninjured arm and stood next to him. He grabbed his other arm again to stop the bleeding. "The man stabbed me. Hurts like bloody hell."

"Then come along." Still carrying Megan, Darnell retraced his steps to the edge of the woods and crossed the clearing to his house, with the Constable following.

As he made the walk, feeling her in his arms, he could not keep his thoughts from going once more to his brother Jeffrey. In carrying her, it was like carrying his brother, saving him, too. He felt a relief in doing it, a warmth that flowed through his system.

Darnell entered through the front door and set Megan on a sofa in the living room, making sure she could not see Stanton's body in the other room. He found a sheet in a cupboard, went into the other room, and covered the body.

With wet cloths and disinfectant, Darnell cleaned Kinney's wound, and put a crude tourniquet on his arm. He was able to reach the local doctor on the telephone, and urged him to come at once to tend to Kinney.

In the kitchen, he discovered provisions Penny had purchased, and brought Megan a glass of milk and a dish of sweet biscuits.

"Now," he said, smiling as he watched her eat, "let's

call your mother and father so you can tell them yourself that you're all right."

Megan smiled. "Yes, please. Hurry."

"After that," he said, "we'll call the Constable's wife, and mine—and then we'll get you a better meal."

Darnell placed the call through Millicent Trelawney, the local operator, and asked to be connected with Prime Minister Lloyd George at Number Ten Downing Street. He had to repeat the name and address to Millicent twice, to be believed.

Chapter 26

Tuesday, December 19, 1916

The train ride from Stow-on-the-Wold to London filled Darnell and Penny with contentment to see the happiness on Megan's face and hear excitement bubbling over in her voice. She talked about her coming reunion with her family.

"Wait'll I tell Mother and Father about all this! And my friends. 'Course, some of it isn't too pleasant, but they'll want to know the lot." She paused, her face serious. "Mr. Stanton was strange. Seemed nice enough at Downing Street. Then kidnapped me. Bought me milk and a sandwich, said he wouldn't kill me. I don't know . . ."

Penny said to her, "My husband said Stanton may have repented."

Darnell smiled grimly. "Those bullets within inches of me didn't show much repentance." He stared out the window at the passing landscape. "But he did give me a message as he died."

Darnell took the girl's hand in his. "I think he wanted me to tell you he was sorry, Megan."

Megan nodded, but said nothing.

Penny touched her shoulder. "You need time to rest now, Megan, and get over your experience. You'll be with your family. And Christmas is coming, too."

Megan smiled. "Going home is my Christmas present, the only one I'll need. The best one I ever had."

Despite the pleasantness of the situation, returning Lloyd George's daughter to him, Darnell had second thoughts about Stanton's death, and his dying words. While Penny and Megan talked about the girl's family, Darnell stared out the window at the passing landscape and reviewed the events of the past few days in his mind. Something bothered him about the neat conclusion of the case, which seemed to end with Stanton's death.

Signs of the outskirts of London were coming into view. "In ten minutes," Darnell said finally, "we'll be at the station."

Penny put her arm around Megan's shoulder. "We'd like to have you come and visit us, have dinner with us sometime."

"I'd like to, after I spend time with my family. They all come down from college—my brothers, Richard and Gwilym, and my sister Olwen. We have little parties, and that."

"So there were five of you children, Mair the oldest?"

She nodded. "I was only seven when Mair died. All of us miss her. I . . . I hoped we could hear her, in the séance, you know. And Father, well, he was desperate to hear her voice. But I'm not sure what I thought. I guess I just wanted to believe it could happen, if he did."

Darnell reflected on her words, and wondered whether they applied to him, also, in his own personal effort to deal with his reopened feelings about Jeffrey.

When they arrived at the station in London, Darnell felt the scene looked like something out of a Dickens novel. Prime Minister Lloyd George and his wife, Margaret, met the Darnells and Megan the moment they stepped out of the railcar. Megan ran into the arms of her mother and they cried on each other's shoulder. Then Lloyd George took Megan in his arms and held her for an even longer time. Tears flowed among them all as they kissed and hugged one another in their great relief. Darnell took Penny's hand as they stood watching the emotional scene.

After a few minutes, Lloyd George tore himself away and wrung Darnell's hand vigorously. "I can't thank you enough, my boy. Anything you ever need, just put a name to it."

Mrs. Lloyd George came over to Darnell and Penny with Megan under her arm. "One thing *I* can supply is an invitation for dinner. Christmas Eve, at Downing Street. All our children will be there."

"It'll be a big party," Lloyd George said. "Scotland Yard people, my War Cabinet, their wives. You'd be an important part of it."

Penny said, "We'd love to come." She glanced at Darnell.

He nodded and smiled. "Yes. In fact, we'd be honored."

After last good-byes and thanks from the Lloyd Georges, the Downing Street driver helped the Prime Minister's family into their car and they drove off.

Darnell and Penny drove home, and when they arrived, Penny exclaimed, "What a welcome sight." They found a warm reception inside from Sung and his son.

Ho San asked, "The girl? She is all right?"

His remark reminded Darnell that the boy was the same age as Megan was. "Yes, she's fine, and with her parents now."

Darnell told them of all the events of the past two days that led to Megan's release. "Now I must make one more call," he said, and walked with Penny into the study, where he placed a call to Scotland Yard. Penny sat near him, listening.

"Megan's at home, Bruce," Darnell said to Chief Inspector Howard.

"Well done! Well done!"

"I want Sergeant O'Reilly to get full credit for her part."

"Agreed. So it's all over now. Time to congratulate ourselves."

"I'm not certain of that."

"But it was Stanton, and his henchmen. No question about that."

"I'm not sure we have them all. There may be someone . . . bigger."

"Do you have any evidence?"

"No, nothing now." He didn't mention the thoughts that nagged him. "Some things I have to look into. By the way, I want to prowl around Stanton's flat."

"The block constable can see to that. It hasn't been disturbed. What's up?"

"I'll tell you later." He hung up the receiver and looked at Penny.

"You have that look about you," she accused. "Are you leaving me again?" She held his hand tightly, as if she wouldn't let him go.

He glanced at his watch. "I have to do a search. I want to hear Lloyd George speak when the Commons reconvenes today. And then I may have another errand or two."

"You'll be back for dinner?"

"Definitely. Plan on it." He took her in his arms for a moment. "We've got a lot of catching up to do."

Darnell had no trouble finding the constable and getting into Stanton's flat. One look, and he thought Charles Dickens would have called the place "unprepossessing." The furniture was nondescript, the view from the single window was a flat brick wall with a weed-ridden courtyard below, and the kitchen constituted a mere alcove the size of the one remaining room—the water closet. The place had a neglected, unlived-in look.

As he poked about the room, he found Stanton's clothes of interest. A dozen suits hung like soldiers in the closet. Two dozen cravats hung on racks, neatly organized by color, and shirts and collars were clean and neatly folded in drawers. He muttered, "A lot of clothes on his salary." He searched the pockets of all the suits and in and under the other clothing, not quite knowing what he was seeking. In the process a picture of Stanton continued to flash through his mind. The wavy brown hair, dark eyebrows, deep-set eyes, and generous mustache. A ladies' man.

Darnell tore into the kitchen alcove and water closet facilities with abandon now, moving things about, overlooking no crevice, convinced Stanton had left some evidence there. He inspected the floor and felt a shock of reward finding a loose board in the corner of the room. Opening it, he took out a white handkerchief, unfolded it, and picked up the contents—an unlabeled key with the number "342" etched into it.

He said the word aloud, "Key," and was reminded of Stanton's last words: ". . . the key." Exhilarated yet still baffled, he replaced the board and stuffed the key in his pocket. He checked his watch and realized he must head for the House of Commons or miss the speech. In minutes his car was clattering in that direction as fast as he could push it.

By the time Darnell entered the visitors' gallery of the House of Commons, he found it already overflowing, with every seat taken and the small standing-room area jammed with observers. The Members of Parliament in their assigned seats, and observers around him, waited with a single desire—to hear what the new Prime Minister would say in his first speech to the House about his new government policies, the conduct of the war, and the German peace proposals.

Darnell, standing in the last row of the gallery, knew that few in the public were aware of the events in the past days since Megan's kidnapping, although some word may have leaked out. The common sentiment he heard expressed about him in gallery conversations was one of curiosity—*"What will he say?"*

More than once he heard others say it had been twelve days since Lloyd George's elevation to Prime

Minister, with no word of policies. "About bloody time," one man whispered to his wife.

The German peace proposals had been disclosed in the press, but since their release on December 12 no intimation had come from Downing Street of the position Lloyd George would express on that most important subject of the day.

A familiar voice at his shoulder said, "Well, Professor, will those mysteries we discussed be resolved today?"

Darnell turned to the speaker, seeing it was Sandy MacDougall, the *London Times* reporter. "Sandy. I should have known you'd be here. You like the gallery-eye view?"

MacDougall nodded. "I get a better feel of what's going on here." He lowered his voice. "So, what's the answer on those mysteries we talked about . . . ?"

Darnell laughed softly. "The Prime Minister will address any issues regarding the war, I'm sure of that."

"And the rest? Come on, John."

"When the time is right. Give me a few days, Sandy."

MacDougall frowned, but said, "All right."

The hall buzzed now with hundreds of conversations, some held in whispers, others more boldly in loud voices, challenging one another, wondering, speculating. In the gallery, Darnell heard other snatches of the conversations: *"Will the war end?" "Will Lloyd George push the war harder, now?"* But in the back of his own mind, another question was pressing on him—*the key.* What did it mean?

Then the Prime Minister suddenly strode into the room, and the amalgam of voices subsided gradually, from what had become a roar, down to a low rumble, as the crowd waited for his first words. He apparently wanted their complete silence, and waited, smiling, waving a hand to one or another in the seats.

No one could say David Lloyd George did not cut a remarkable figure, Darnell thought, as he watched the drama. He was a different man here today. The

Prime Minister's white mane of hair seemed to sweep back like that of a silver lion and evoke the strength of that awesome beast. His white brush mustache seemed to bristle even more than usual. His heeled boots had clacked on the floor as he entered.

The power of his personage and personality was evident in Lloyd George's proud strike from the moment he had entered the room, in his trademark vested suit with a large bow tie against his wing-tip collar, and the ever-present white linen handkerchief in his pocket.

On Darnell's right, a white-haired woman said, "He's such a handsome man." But the man next to her responded, "He's just a dandy."

A "dandy" Lloyd George might be, Darnell thought, but no one presented a more powerful image and force than he when on the political stage.

Darnell listened to the applause in the House and watched the Prime Minister in the realization that the man had a strength much greater this day than he had possessed just the day before, when his daughter was in the hands and at the mercy of those he would no doubt speak against now.

Darnell could see Lloyd George was about to retain his deserved reputation as one of the greatest orators of his time, and, with his energy and confidence restored, would be at the height of his powers. "Get your pencil and notebook ready, Sandy," he said to the reporter at his side. "History is about to be made."

Lloyd George bowed slightly and stood looking and smiling at the crowd. Now Darnell watched him step forward, dropping a large book on the podium in front of him.

Seeing he was ready to speak, the crowd settled quickly into an observant and respectful silence. But when the Prime Minister opened with "My right honorable friends . . . ," loud applause broke out for long, seemingly endless minutes.

Darnell joined the applause until it at last subsided. The Parliament members and audience reverted to an attentive posture.

Lloyd George opened with thanks for his new position as Prime Minister, and pledging his best. Then his voice became more strident with his words "Now, consider the so-called peace proposals from Germany. What are their proposals? There are none, really. They would simply end the war with a conference, with terms yet to be named, and with Germany proclaiming itself victorious without any concessions. We cannot end this hated blood-soaked war that way, without achieving our objectives. We must have complete restitution, full reparation, and effectual guarantees!"

The Members interrupted his words with applause, and there was a call for order. Ringing in Darnell's mind was Lloyd George's word "victorious." He began thinking of his own problem, how to achieve success in his own way, and his mind started to come into focus on it. But his attention was drawn back to Lloyd George's speech as the crowd settled down again.

Lloyd George continued. "The Allies joined together in this war to defend against Prussian aggression and military domination of Europe, and we cannot end it without the most complete and effective guarantee against them ever again disturbing the peace of Europe again. Even as Germans speak of peace, their merciless submarines mount unrestricted warfare against our merchant shipping and imports of food and supplies to our people. In the face of this inhumanity by a brutal adversary, we must not yield!"

Applause and shouts of support frequently interrupted his fiery remarks. Darnell heard them with one part of his consciousness while the other dwelt on his own mystery.

Lloyd George went on. "The Germans cannot be lightly trusted. To enter a conference without knowing the terms is to put our heads into a noose with the rope end in the hands of Germany." He shook his head. "We will wait for the German government to offer specific terms and guarantees. Meanwhile, we

shall put our trust in our valiant soldiers and our un-
broken army, rather than holding our faith in devious
German diplomats, and false and broken German
promises. I stand for rejection of the proposals, and I
urge you to stand with me. And for England."

Members in the House and observers in the gallery
applauded in a standing ovation, the sound and length
of which few observers had ever heard or seen. Sandy
MacDougall tucked his pencil in his pocket, smiled at
Darnell, and joined the applause.

Prime Minister David Lloyd George's face beamed
as he offered his smile about the room, with flashing
eyes and jutting chin. The lion of politics still reigned
supreme. Confident and inspiring. The king of his
Commons.

Darnell whirled about even as the applause continued, and elbowed his way out of the gallery, bolting
down the steps and out to the street, to his car. His
thoughts had jelled. He knew what to do now, and his
destination was but a mile away. In minutes he
reached it, parked, and ran into the huge building.
Looking about, he stopped at the information desk,
and, given the information he wanted, he rushed to a
far end of the cavernous room.

The large bank of lockers faced him as he ran up,
and he quickly found number 342 and inserted the
key. It opened. Inside, he saw what he had hoped
would be there—an envelope that obviously contained
some sheets of paper. He removed it and stuffed it in
his pocket. He glanced about nervously, as if expecting
to see someone observing him, and then ran back out
to his car. Inside, he tore open the envelope and de-
voured the words on the three pages. They told him
everything he wanted to know. Now to go to Scotland
Yard. He cranked the starter.

As he drove back around the building, a wry smile
twisted his lips when he glanced at the sign: "Victoria Station."

*   *   *

Darnell headed straight for Chief Inspector Howard's office at the Yard and, reaching it, closed the door behind him as he entered and sat in front of Howard's desk, favoring the white-haired Chief Inspector with a broad smile. "I've got it! The evidence I knew was out there, somewhere."

Howard's eyes widened. "Well, don't hold back now. Read it, man!" Which Darnell proceeded to do.

He read aloud Stanton's words, written over a two-week period, describing the planning of Megan's kidnapping, obtaining Baldrik and the others, the arguments over the proposed killing of Brent and his eventual death, and, in almost every line, implicating the person responsible for it all. The papers were dated and signed, Hugo Stanton.

"This is it, then. We'll tell Lloyd George, and pick him up."

Darnell shook his head. "No. I've thought of our next steps, driving over here. The man has to implicate himself to make it iron-clad. Otherwise the courts might just say it's Stanton's words—even though they are equivalent to dying words—against his."

Howard scratched his head. "What, then?"

"The Prime Minister is holding a big party of celebration on Christmas Eve at Downing Street. We can get what we need there, and come away with a good case. But we must not tell Lloyd George about it. Only four people can know. You and I and Conan Doyle. And, of course, the fourth, but most critical one in the whole scenario . . ."

Howard looked at him and frowned. Darnell's propensity for the dramatic was well known. "All right, John . . ."

Darnell smiled. "Madame Ilena Ispenska."

Chapter 27

Wednesday, December 20, 1916

Madame Ilena Ispenska faced Chief Inspector Bruce Howard, Conan Doyle, and Professor John Darnell across the table in Inspector Howard's office. She knew these three men could determine whether she spent years in a musty jail cell, or free to live her life as she saw fit. She felt intimidated by them. In her heart, she did not believe she deserved to be treated as a criminal, but how to persuade them of that was the question.

Inspector Howard glared at her and said, "Kidnapping. Murder. Treason. Tell me why we shouldn't just clap you in irons, toss you in prison, and throw away the key."

Doyle and Darnell exchanged wry glances but said nothing.

Madame Ispenska drew herself up straight in the chair. She promised herself, *I won't beg, no matter what they do.* Aloud, she said, "I did none of those, Chief Inspector. I did not help in the kidnapping, I was shocked by the murder, and I am a patriot."

Seeing no change in their expressions, she urged, "I am innocent, I swear!" Seeing him glare without responding, she added, "I . . . I know I make some mistakes. Not all my fault. I was deceived. I am still a . . . a woman, after all."

"And what would that mean?"

"Stanton. How can I say it? He was the chief aide to the Prime Minister. He was impressive. He gave me the work, he was the one paid me for it. Then, the night before the séance, he comes to me and . . . no other way to say it, he seduces me."

Howard tugged at his collar, and cleared his throat. "Well, on the facts, madame. You're telling me you knew nothing about the plan to kidnap Megan when the lights were out?"

"No, nothing."

"What *did* Stanton ask you to do?" Howard's voice had taken on an edge.

She smoothed her long hair back with jerky, repetitive motions. "He told me the Prime Minister must hear Mair's voice. I should be sure the Prime Minister hears something, anything, from her. I agreed. But my trance was broken, and the session ended. Then we heard they'd try again, and he said to say I could do it, that I would try again."

"And in the second séance, you did exactly . . . what?"

"I knew I had a problem, because I wasn't sure of my powers in the presence of all those powerful men. The Prime Minister, so powerful just by himself, made me nervous. But it was all right—I was able to go into a trance. They say that words coming from my mouth sounded like the daughter's."

"You don't know?"

She rolled her eyes upward. "When I am in trance, I hear nothing. When I wake, I know nothing of what happened."

"You expect me to believe Mair's voice was heard by them."

"They say that." She looked at Doyle, who nodded.

"Folderol! I've never heard such nonsense." Chief Inspector Howard tossed his pencil down on the desk.

Conan Doyle's face flushed. "Look here, Chief Inspector, you may not believe in spiritualism, but millions of people rely on it now. All over the world."

Howard shook his head. "But there are fakes, charlatans."

"Of course, there are some. But I, myself, have had experiences that were genuine, things that affected me personally, in séances I attended." Doyle sniffed. "The kind of things, of course, that *you* wouldn't believe, unless you opened your mind."

"You're right about that." Howard turned to Darnell. "John?"

"I won't comment on the séances. But Madame Ispenska—she helped me personally at the prisoner house, giving me the clue that Stanton would be going after Penny." He looked at the medium. "I owe her immeasurable thanks for that."

Howard scowled. "Well, that's true. And she was a prisoner when you found her." He drummed his fingers on his desk, and turned to the medium. "Under the circumstances, with these two gentlemen vouching for you . . ."

Madame Ispenska smiled, a heavy load seeming to be lifted from her shoulders. "I can go?"

"Ye-es." He looked at her over the tops of his glasses with a half smile. "But stay out of trouble, Madame. There are laws against fraud, you know. You'll be looking out through iron bars if you break them."

Ilena Ispenska's mind flashed back to her own father, who often argued with her and with her mother about their beliefs and practices in the same way, over the tops of his glasses, as Howard did. She sighed, rose, and bowed to Doyle and Darnell.

To Howard, she said, "Yes, sir," and inclined her head, a small bow of acceptance, just as she often had done to her father, accepting the power shown to her, but without yielding her own integrity. Her mind, she vowed, would always be her own private territory. She could let him believe she bowed to his authority, if it helped secure her freedom. "Then I go to my home. I have moved back into it."

But the medium knew she couldn't let it end there.

She looked back at the three men. "I have something to say. Soldiers come back from war now, and there will be many of them, poor boys. They recover from wounds, but cannot forget their comrades who died at their side. I will help them, in hospitals, in rehabilitation homes, in their own homes, to reach their comrades. I can give them comfort. And I will do it. With my séances."

Madame Ispenska turned, swept her shawl over her shoulder, and walked to the door, chin high, with an inner satisfaction, and with her integrity intact.

"Madame, wait," the Chief Inspector called. He stood and walked over to her. "We have more to say—Professor Darnell, that is. He will speak to you privately in our conference room."

The medium looked at Darnell, who nodded reassuringly. "I will wait."

Howard opened the door and motioned to an officer. "Take Madame Ispenska to the conference room and make her comfortable—tea, coffee, you know." He nodded at her and she followed the officer down the hallway.

Closing the door behind her, Howard shook his head and chuckled. "That's one very determined woman. I didn't scare her much. Didn't try real hard."

Doyle said, "She won't break any laws, Chief Inspector. And she has a point. You must accept that séances are a private issue, not a police matter."

"And I need her for this final step," Darnell said.

"No harm done. I agree she's no danger." Howard studied Doyle. "Do you think she's legitimate, that she can do any of what she claims?"

"She's had success, I know it."

Darnell asked Howard, "How is Sergeant O'Reilly?"

"She'll leave the hospital tomorrow, and be back to work in a few days."

Darnell nodded. "I'll stop by and see her later—but

first, Madame Ispenska. I'll go over with her everything I told you."

Darnell entered the conference room and sat opposite Madame Ispenska at the small oval table. She looked at him with obvious curiosity.

"I'll come straight to the point, Madame. You are in a position to be of immense help to Scotland Yard in helping to punish those responsible for these recent events, including your own imprisonment."

"Responsible? But Stanton is dead."

"Someone else gave him his orders. He must be punished. We must see that he can do no more damage to the country or any of its citizens."

She frowned. "But who are we talking of?"

Without disclosing the man's name, Darnell read the pages recounting in detail the conspiracy, the criminal history of the men who imprisoned Megan, and the plan to kill Robert Brent. Several times Madame Ispenska shook her head or sucked in her breath. At the end of the last page she looked up at Darnell. "This is no man. This is an animal. An animal to be butchered."

"We need your help." He paused. "There may be danger."

She waved a hand dismissively. "I have seen danger. Just tell me what to do."

"The Prime Minister is holding a great party on Christmas Eve. All his family, Scotland Yard people, the War Cabinet and wives, and my wife and I. And you. That is where you can help."

She waved a hand in impatience. "Tell me. I listen."

"We want to have one last séance, to have you conduct it, and have it work to our purposes, to cement our case against this man. He will be at the party, and we have an expectation as to what he will do, but much depends on you."

"Professor, I told Chief Inspector Howard I am a patriot. This is my adopted country, and this will give me a chance to prove how I feel. Tell me. I will do what you wish."

The air in the corridor of the Royal Hospital bore pungent odors of disinfectant and ammonia cleaning products, blended with a faint residue of stale urine. Darnell wondered how patients could ever get back to health with such air to breathe for days.

After the nurse warned Sergeant O'Reilly she had a visitor and cleared the way for him to enter her hospital room, Darnell poked his head around the corner of her door. "Hello, Sergeant."

Catherine O'Reilly beamed at him. "Come in, John. So glad you're here." She was propped up in bed, her head still swathed in bandages.

Darnell realized it was the first time he'd seen her out of the Yard's Sergeant's uniform. The bed jacket draped around her shoulders made her look younger and more vulnerable.

"Come, sit by the bed."

He took the chair next to the bed, reached over the steel railing, and touched her hand. "So, they're letting you out soon."

She smiled. "I'm hard to kill. But tell me about the case, John. I want to know everything."

Darnell picked up the story at the point where she had been shot at the prisoner house, describing events in the Cotswolds, and Lloyd George's speech. He held back on the final plan.

When he finished, she smiled. "You've been busy, John."

He handed her the day's *London Times,* and pointed to the article on page one. "Here's something more important. The whole story's in the press today. You're a celebrity again. Just like last year when you saved the son of that actress."

She scanned the words and looked up at him, frowning. "But, John, I didn't have this much to do with it. It was you . . ."

Darnell shook his head. "I won't hear that. Besides, there's plenty of praise to go around. And it's free."

She gazed off in space for a moment. "I always knew making me the first woman Sergeant at Scotland Yard was an experiment, and that I could easily be put back down on the street. In fact, they kept my status quite a secret from the city, certainly didn't publicize it. But I guess I'll keep my stripes now."

Darnell said, "Women will become more and more valuable in police work, and in other fields. I read that they'll have a female surgeon at this very hospital within a year, and a woman as King's Counsel at the Old Bailey the year after. Why not a female Scotland Yard Sergeant?" His eyes twinkled. "And someday— maybe Detective Sergeant."

She laughed, and put a hand on his. "Thanks, John. I need a lot of support, like all women these days."

He stood. "I enjoyed working with you. Maybe we'll work together again, Sergeant . . . Catherine."

She smiled. "I hope so."

They said their good-byes, and Darnell took the stairs two at a time down to the lobby, anxious to be out of the building. Outside, he strode down the sidewalk toward his car, filling his lungs with each step.

"Ah!" he breathed. "Fresh air!"

Chapter 28

The telephone rang as soon as Darnell closed the door to his flat. He called to Sung, who was walking toward the sitting room, "I'll get it, Sung."

He scooped up the phone in the sitting room on the third ring. "Darnell," he said into it.

"Thank God you're there, John!" Chief Inspector Howard's voice carried as much agitation as Darnell had heard in it at any point in the case. "He's escaped!"

"Escaped? Who?" Darnell's mind raced. It must be—a face flashed in his mind.

"The second kidnapper. The one called Baldrik. We had him under guard at the Royal Hospital. He's gone. God knows where."

"I just left the hospital, but I'll come right back. My God! O'Reilly's there."

He dashed back through the entry and out the door to his car. As he drove off, he saw Sung and Penny standing at the open door, looking after him. He waved. No time to explain, now.

Darnell heard the commotion even as he turned the corner a half block from the hospital. Several police cars were pulled in at odd angles at the entrance. A half dozen uniformed officers stood near the cars, and others were stationed at the side doors and back entrances of the building.

Chief Inspector Howard's white hair and stocky physique stood out in the crowd, at the hospital front doorway. He was huddled with what were apparently some plainclothes detectives, and was apparently issuing orders. Darnell parked his car and ran up to them.

"What's the latest?" he asked.

"We're going up to the second floor," the Inspector said. "Baldrik's whereabouts was just discovered, and I'm afraid it's bad news, John."

Darnell had a dread foreboding as he asked, "What is it?"

"The man's got Sergeant O'Reilly in her hospital room. He was able to get a knife somewhere, apparently one of those big postmortem instruments. And he's holding her captive with it." He wiped his forehead. "I don't think he'd hesitate to use it."

"I was afraid of that, but didn't want to admit it to myself. Sergeant O'Reilly! Too bad that scum didn't die with the other one. What are your plans?"

"I'll talk to him, first. Come on." Howard led the way, running through the double doors, down the hall, then up the stairs. Darnell ran at his side, two detectives and two uniformed officers following them a few feet back.

At O'Reilly's hospital room, Howard stopped to catch his breath and looked in through the open door. It was exactly as his men had described to him minutes before. Baldrik stood to one side of the bed holding a large knife to O'Reilly's throat.

Howard called out. "All right, Baldrik. The hospital's surrounded. Give it up now and no harm will come to you."

Baldrik barked a harsh laugh. "No harm?" he said. "Harm is what it's all about, copper. Harm to your friend here. Your lovely little Sergeant. But she won't be so lovely if I don't get out of here."

In a low voice, Darnell said to Howard, "We're talking about her life here. Ask him what he wants."

Howard nodded, whispering, "I've been through this kind of thing before." He called to Baldrik, "We can make some arrangements, a deal."

"A deal? Hah!" Baldrik paused, seeming to think it over for a moment. "All right—here's my deal. A car at the door, full of gas, and no police cars, no bloody coppers around. I take her with me. Nobody buggers me, nobody follows me. When I'm sure I'm clear, I drop her off."

"Don't be a fool, man. We can't let you kidnap a police officer."

Baldrik growled. "I'm not asking you to let me, I'm telling you that's what happens if you want her alive. And I'm giving you just ten minutes to do it. The clock on the wall in here says five past three. You got till fifteen past. So get cracking!"

Howard moved away from the door and scowled at Darnell. "We don't have any choice, dammit! I can't bluff him. And Catherine's more important than he is."

Howard turned to his detectives. "All right, you heard it. Scott, clear the hallways of nurses and doctors—this isn't a side show. Jimmy, move those cars away from the entrance, send all the uniforms out of the hospital and a block away. Put one unmarked car near the door, make sure it's gassed up. And one of you get back up here and tell me when it's ready. You've got ten minutes!"

Inspector Howard motioned Darnell to walk down the hall a few paces with him, out of earshot of Baldrik. "God, I hate to give in to him," Howard said.

Darnell looked up and down the hall. One of the detectives was already ordering nurses, doctors, and service personnel into their offices.

"I've got an idea," Darnell said, and ran down the corridor.

Howard shook his head, and stepped back to the doorway to O'Reilly's room. He called in to Baldrik. "We're doing what you said. It'll take at least the ten minutes. I'll let you know."

"Don't stall, copper. Or your Sergeant will be getting another stripe. Around her neck."

Each minute on the wall clock clicked over slowly and noisily. In the now breathless interval, Chief Inspector Howard waited impatiently for his men to complete the preparations he'd ordered. He heard, and counted, each click of the clock, one by one.

Darnell ran down the stairwell with one of the hospital service personnel he had commandeered. When they reached the main floor, he demanded, "Where's that room you said was down here?"

The man gestured. "Just to your left, guv'nor. There."

The two ducked into the room and closed the door. Inside, Darnell pointed at the garments the man was wearing and said, "Get out a set of those that'll fit me." He pulled off his outer clothing as the janitor brought him a denim work shirt and a pair of blue coveralls. He pulled them on and dropped his 38 into a pocket. "Now work shoes, and a bucket and a mop."

The other man produced the equipment.

Darnell pulled on the heavy shoes. "Put some water in that bucket and some soap. Make it look like it usually does when you do your work."

The janitor complied.

"Now, listen," Darnell said. "You stay in here. I can't have you out there, in danger. Keep this door closed, because the killer will be passing right by you." He grabbed a cap hanging just inside the door and pulled it on his head. He opened the door, looked both ways, closed it behind him, and strode down the hall toward the front entrance.

He turned into a right-angled corridor leading out to the entrance and took a position against the right wall. He sloshed the water across the floor, bent over, and swished the mop about, keeping the bucket nearby. His head was down but he watched the hallway to his left, and listened.

One of the detectives ran past him and up the stairs. They had carried out the procedures. It was beginning.

Darnell tried to imagine the scene upstairs. Baldrik holding one arm around O'Reilly, the knife in the other, walking her down the corridor, then pushing her down the stairwell. Now he heard the sound of footsteps coming toward him in the main hall. In a moment they would round the corner in his direction. And he would have his one chance. He kept his head down over the floor and grabbed the bucket in one hand.

Baldrik turned the corner, holding the Sergeant with his left arm, as Darnell had imagined, his right hand holding the long knife to her throat. As they approached, Baldrik burst out, "Damned janitor, water all over the place."

Darnell looked up and directly into O'Reilly's eyes, hoping she would recognize him. If only . . . Yes, she did see him!

The Sergeant did what he expected. She leaned backward away from the knife and jabbed an elbow into Baldrik's face. Darnell jumped forward as she pulled to one side, away from both of them. Baldrik saw Darnell now, recognized him, and raised the knife in the air as Darnell ran forward. Darnell swung the bucket hard at Baldrik's arm and knocked the knife down the hallway.

Darnell dropped the bucket, which clanged on the hard floor, and continued his forward movement, charging the man, not caring that Baldrik's head was still bandaged from the earlier gunshot wound. Fairness was not an issue. He crashed forward into Baldrik, and with the momentum of his run carried them both banging into the far wall.

Baldrik's head struck the hard wall and he gave a cry of pain and anger that echoed down the corridor. Darnell hit him on the point of the jaw with all his strength, and felt the jar in his knuckles. When he heard the crunch of the other's jaw from the blow, and the sound of Baldrik's head cracking on the floor as he fell, he knew it was all over.

Chief Inspector Howard and his detective rounded

the corner at a full run and pulled up short at the scene. Howard picked up the knife. "Put the irons on him, Scott. Both hands, both feet. Then have this garbage carried out to the car."

Sergeant O'Reilly threw her arms around Darnell and sobbed, "Thank God!" but then she quickly broke away, embarrassed.

Darnell said, "I'm glad you recognized me in these clothes."

O'Reilly rubbed her elbow and looked up at him. "And if I hadn't seen you, John? What would you have done?"

He shook his head. "I wasn't thinking that far ahead. I knew I could count on you to throw him off balance. That was vital. I couldn't let him take you, of course. He would have killed you when you'd served his purposes."

Chief Inspector Howard walked over to them. "Well, that was damn-blasted, bloody foolhardy of you, John." He held out his big, gnarled hand and shook Darnell's. He smiled broadly. "But I'm glad you did it." They watched his men carrying the still-unconscious Baldrik out through the double doors to the cars. "He'll hang now, for sure. I'll see to it."

Outside, Baldrik's voice shouted obscenities. He had come to his senses.

Darnell gestured at the mop and bucket. "That was the first time I ever used a bucket as a weapon."

"And the last, I expect," O'Reilly said. She smiled. "But those overalls really do something for you, John. You should add a pair to your wardrobe."

That night, as Darnell and Penny finished dinner, she said, "Only five days until Christmas, John. Your case is settled at last, and you have no other big ones pending." Penny frowned. "Or . . . are there?"

Darnell laughed. "Nothing that can't wait until after the holidays. And my classes are adjourned until January. We'll have this time together."

Sung came in on the end of the conversation and

grinned. "I fix big dinner for Christmas Day. A goose. One thing English and Chinese have in common, both like goose."

"No Chinese delicacies?" Darnell looked at him.

He shook his head. "English plum pudding."

Penny smiled. "You know we'll be at Downing Street on Christmas Eve, Sung. No need to cook for that night."

"I know. Tell them I cook the goose for Christmas. They could have prime rib, perhaps?" He bowed lightly.

John Darnell laughed. "Prime Minister, prime rib! I'll tell them your joke."

As Sung removed the dishes, the Darnells strolled to the sitting room. Penny said, "We must take a present for Megan."

Darnell said, "Yes, I'll leave that to you."

They took seats on the sofa to await the coffee Sung would bring in soon. The fire Sung had lit crackled in the fireplace. Penny clicked off the lamp, throwing the room into semidarkness, illuminated only by the flickering flames.

"There'll be a surprise at the dinner party."

Penny smiled at Darnell. "Then tell me, and it won't be a surprise."

"There will be one final séance. An important one. You'll be able to sit in on it, along with everyone else."

Her unlined forehead creased as she looked at him. "I think, John, there's more to it than what you're telling me."

"Wear your best séance dress."

She laughed. "I see that's all I'm going to get out of you."

The talk of séances brought back to Darnell's mind the private one Madame Ispenska had performed for him at her house that midnight. And the words of his brother Jeffrey that seemed to emanate from her mouth in a child's voice. He couldn't believe it had happened, and yet such an experience struck at the core of his psyche and belief system, the foundation of his paranormal investigations.

Penny sighed, laid her head on his shoulder, and said, "John, you seem preoccupied. Relax, dear."

He stared into the fireplace. Soon he would open those wounds for the last time, tell Penny of the séance, and what he might have heard there. And hope she could help him sort it out.

Chapter 29

Sunday night, December 24, 1916

Prime Minister David Lloyd George stood and raised his glass. "A very merry Christmas to you all!" He beamed at those seated at the extended-length dining table.

On his right sat his smiling wife and his four children, Olwen, Gwilym, Richard, and Megan. Beyond them were Penny and John Darnell, Conan Doyle and his wife, Chief Inspector Howard, and Sergeant Catherine O'Reilly. On the opposite side sat his War Cabinet members—Addison, Curzon, Milner, Law, and Adler, and the wives of three of them. The Prime Minister remained standing as they all clinked glasses and sipped of the wine.

"This Christmas could have been the worst one of our lives, since Mair died. But thanks to our guests, Professor Darnell, Sergeant O'Reilly, and my good friend Conan Doyle, we're all here together, safe and sound. We know, too, the danger Mrs. Darnell faced." He paused and looked directly at Darnell. "With your help, John, I was saved from dealing with those atrocious peace proposals in some ignominious way. Now we can go on to victory with clear consciences and new determination."

Lloyd George took his seat as conversation buzzed again while the roast beef was being carved and York-

shire pudding and vegetables and breads were served
by the attending waiters. They all busied themselves
with their food, and, after dishes were cleared, rasp-
berry trifle was served, along with coffee.

Darnell, seated next to Lloyd George, said to him,
"Prime Minister, one thing bothers me. The peace
proposals. Many men will die, now that the war will
continue."

"That was a state decision, John. Many have died,
many more will. But we have to do what's right. You
gave me the chance to make that decision with a clear
mind, having my daughter back with me again. But it
was my choice alone."

"And the war? How will it be affected?"

"Your help in this, and my declining the proposals,
may actually turn the tide of the war toward success.
America will join the Allies, now that the war continues. That will insure that we achieve a decisive victory,
and hopefully sooner."

Darnell considered the Prime Minister's remarks.
"Do you feel, Prime Minister, as I do, the futility of
this war? We see false pride, overconfidence, and
thoughtlessness. I hope the war ends soon, but I'm
wondering . . . will the outcome be simply to topple
a few decadent monarchies in Europe, decimate an
entire generation of young men, and sow seeds for
future wars?"

Lloyd George's jaw was set firm. "I know what you
mean. Some say this is a war to end all war, until the
next one. But we'll have peace conferences after we
win, and ironbound treaties. We'll do what we can to
insure peace. Yet, until the day when people of the
world see they all have common needs for survival
and progress, man's driving compulsion to wage war
for principles may still win out from time to time over
his innate desire for a peaceful existence. It's the nature of humankind."

Darnell said, "Let's hope that day comes in our
lifetimes."

Lloyd George said, "Yes . . . and let's talk of more

pleasant things." He pulled an envelope from his pocket and handed it to Darnell. "For saving my daughter, and for helping your country."

Darnell opened the envelope and glanced at the bank draft inside. His lips formed in a silent whistle. "Very generous, Prime Minister."

"Think of me now as David, your friend. What you have in your hand shows how much we were indebted to you. It's my small way of trying to repay our debt."

When Lloyd George turned away and engaged in conversation with others, Penny seized the opportunity to speak with her husband. "John, there's something I've been wanting to tell you for a half hour. Listen to me."

"Of course, what is it?"

She spoke in a whisper. "Don't look at him, but notice that man across from me. I've seen him before, and the memory isn't good. I'm trying to think where."

Darnell nodded and unobtrusively eyed the man. "All right, dear. Think about it. But I wouldn't advise talking with him about that, or anything else, really. Not just now. Engage in talk with the children, perhaps."

She took the cue and began speaking with Megan.

When brandy was brought out for the men, Lloyd George stood again and cleared his throat. "Now, I think Conan Doyle has a little surprise for us." He looked at Doyle and took his seat.

Doyle stood and took a deep breath. "We're going to have another séance."

The others exchanged looks of surprise and astonishment. Law and Adler exchanged glances, and Addison leaned over and asked Law, "Did you know about this, Bonar?"

Law said, "No. I hope Lloyd George knows what he's doing."

Adler scowled. "This is getting tedious, that Doyle . . ."

Doyle went on. "I know what you're all thinking,

but we have guards posted tonight. There's no chance of anything happening this time." He stepped to the door and opened it. In the hall, facing the dining room, stood Madame Ilena Ispenska, dressed in fine silks. Her long hair streamed behind her and her deep eyes stared at the group. She bowed low and said, "Good evening."

Lloyd George said, "Arthur has arranged one last séance in the other room. At this season, he feels we might have success." He stood. "Now, just follow me to the other room."

He stood and offered his arm to his wife. They walked out into the hall and turned toward the other room.

The others exchanged looks of awe for a moment, until Megan said, "I'm not afraid. Let's go." She marched through the door following her father and mother.

Lloyd George's War Cabinet members followed her. The other children and guests followed. Darnell walked next to Doyle and whispered to him, "Arthur, are you sure Madame knows what to do?"

Doyle nodded his head vigorously. "I've gone over it with her, word for word. Just as you said. No chance of any problem. It's under control. Sergeant O'Reilly and Chief Inspector Howard are here, and the other men are ready for anything."

When Darnell reached the room, he found that the red bulb the medium used had been installed already, giving the room that dim red glow that he had come to know mediums felt was always necessary for their proper communion with spirits.

Penny whispered, "I can't believe it, John. Is it safe, after everything you told me happened?"

He nodded. "You'll understand everything, when it's over."

Everyone took seats at the circular table. At Madame Ispenska's urging, they held the hand of the neighbor on either side of them. Margaret sat at Lloyd

George's right, and Doyle at his left, next to the medium.

Catherine O'Reilly, at Darnell's left, said, close to his ear, "Last time we began this way we ended up with a dead body."

In a low voice Darnell said, "Just stay alert."

Madame Ispenska said, "Quiet now. I try for my trance." She closed her eyes and leaned her head backward. The room was dark and so quiet the medium's heavy breathing could be heard by all. Minutes passed. At last, Madame Ispenska's voice spoke in a monotone. "Robert, Robert Brent, talk to us."

The room buzzed with exclamations and expressions of surprise. When it subsided, the room again lapsed into quiet, and all conversation ended. Soon, Madame Ispenska began to moan softly. The sound reverberated throughout the room, and Darnell felt Penny's body stiffen and her hand tighten in his.

More minutes passed. The medium's moan continued, until, abruptly, she jerked back in her chair and spoke halting, words, not in her own voice, but in a man's voice, sad and sepulchral:

"He murdered me . . ."

"It's Robert!" said Lloyd George's wife. There was a sharp intake of breath among the others.

". . . because I uncovered his secrets," the voice went on. *"Kidnapper—murderer—traitor, you must pay . . ."*

Chairs scraped on the floor and there was movement about the table. Darnell peered into the red gloom. Doyle whispered, "It's happening."

"I will name my killer . . ."

Running footsteps sounded on the hard floor.

"Now!" Darnell shouted, and bright lights flood the room.

Charles Adler was running toward Ilena Ispenska, arm outstretched with a knife in hand. Darnell bolted toward the man and grappled with him. In a moment Chief Inspector Howard was in the midst of it also, grabbing Adler's other arm. The knife dropped and

Adler fell to the floor from one of Darnell's blows. A
torrent of profanity flowed from his lips.

"That'll be enough of that," Howard said, and
clapped handcuffs on Adler's wrists behind the man's
back. "Sergeant O'Reilly, call in two constables
quickly. We have an enemy of the state here, and a
cowardly murderer."

Madame Ispenska seemed to come out of her trance
promptly, eyes clear and voice steady. "You have
him? Good."

Penny Darnell grabbed Doyle's arm. "That man,
now I remember. I have to tell John."

"Wait a moment—he's about to say something."

The constables stood at the sides of Adler, one of
his arms secured by each of them.

Lloyd George said, with evident total astonishment
and a bit of pique, "It's time for an explanation,
Professor."

Darnell faced the Prime Minister, and behind him
the visage of Charles Adler, held in custody, yet with
eyes still glaring with hate at Darnell.

"When Stanton died, right at my feet, he said a few
words that I didn't understand at the time. He said,
'. . . victory . . . the key . . .' I thought he was referring
to that desperate cause he was dedicated to, victory
for the German Empire. But the key to what? European solidarity? I went to his flat and searched it from
top to bottom. And then, under a loose piece of floor-
ing in an unused corner, I found it. A key. Stanton
had referred to a key. 'The key,' he said—but an actual key, not a metaphorical one."

Darnell looked directly at Lloyd George. "Then the
meaning of his other word crystalized as I heard your
speech, Prime Minister, and you said, 'victorious.'
Stanton wasn't trying to say 'victory,' but actually 'Victoria,' for Victoria Station. And I knew then the key
I had would open some kind of storage box there. The
tag had been removed. But the number was clear. So
I went to the station, and—cutting through the rest of

the story—I found the box, opened it, and retrieved these."

Darnell removed the sheets of paper from his coat pocket and held them out. "These implicate Charles Adler as the chief conspirator in this whole plot to kidnap Megan and force the Prime Minister to accept the German peace proposals. The murder of the unfortunate Robert Brent by Adler is documented here also. Brent had overheard Adler's voice speaking in German on the phone, enough to know Adler was the criminal mind behind everything. He would have gone to the Prime Minister after the second séance. But he didn't live to do so."

When voices broke out in a loud buzz, Penny stepped to Darnell's side and whispered in his ear. What he heard made him glare directly at Adler. He held up his hand to quiet the noise. "My wife tells me, as added evidence, that Charles Adler was the man who gave instructions to the two hoodlums who threatened her with a knife after the charity affair. She can identify him."

"That's enough," Chief Inspector Howard said. "Take him away."

The constables took Adler from the room. Lloyd George and the other cabinet members gathered around Darnell, and the Prime Minister said, "I had a momentary doubt, John, but now—well, we must simply thank you again. It's incredible that he was the one, but thank God you found him out."

Lloyd George stepped over to his wife and put an arm around her shoulder. Their four children came to their sides in a rush, and formed a loose circle about them. Megan reached out for her father's hand.

After a round of good-byes and congratulations, the guests drifted away quickly, leaving Chief Inspector Howard, Sergeant O'Reilly, Sir Arthur Conan Doyle and his wife, Madame Ispenska, and John and Penny Darnell the last to leave.

As they took their leave and said good nights to the Prime Minister, Darnell turned to Conan Doyle with a grim smile. "I think Downing Street," he said, "has had its last séance."

The group stood outside the Prime Minister's residence waiting for cars to be brought around. Darnell and the medium stood aside as the others talked, some steps away. His eyes bored into hers. "You seemed to be in a trance, as we planned. Does that mean you have faked every other séance you've conducted?"

She shook her head. "Certainly not. You asked me to help you this time, and I did it. Brent did not have a deep voice, and I could match it, and did. With reluctance. The other times—I deceived no one. I was always in my trance, Professor. I told you that, and those present at a séance have to decide what they heard."

Darnell frowned as he asked a personal question that had been nagging him. "And Jeffrey? That night at your house."

"The same. You must decide whether it was real to you. All I say is that I do not deceive anyone to hurt them. But there is one thing I will tell you. Just before the second séance here at Downing Street, when you and Sir Arthur Conan Doyle were talking . . ."

"Yes?" Darnell's eyes narrowed, as he thought back to the scene. "Go on."

"You mentioned to him a disappearance of your young brother Jeffrey."

He scowled. "You heard. So your claim of contacting Jeffrey, that was all a fake?"

"That is not what I'm saying. I just want you to know I knew of him from your conversation. It was a knowledge in my consciousness. But I was in a trance, and what happened and what you heard, I leave to you to decide for yourself, because I don't know what I said. Whatever I said, I stand by. But the fact that I knew about Jeffrey may help you to sleep better, if you want it to. Now you have a reason to *disbelieve* in me, if you want to. It is up to you."

"You're saying the reality of it is what I perceive."

She smiled. "Exactly. Whatever you have felt in your heart since then, Professor, and feel now, and feel in the future. That is the important thing."

She turned toward the official car as a driver brought it around and stepped out to open the door for her. "Remember. Your belief, or disbelief, decides your own truth. And that's true with every séance, every effort to reach departed souls, by me or anyone else."

She stepped into the car and the driver quickly drove off. Darnell watched the car until it turned the corner, then joined the others.

Penny took his arm. "What was that all about, dear?"

"A meeting of the minds, you might say."

He turned to Conan Doyle. "What now for you, Arthur?"

"Glad you asked," Doyle said, and pulled a bulky envelope from his pocket. He extracted several photographs and handed them to Darnell, who held the photographs up to catch the light of the lamppost. The others peered at the photos with widening eyes. Doyle's wife stood apart, silent.

Darnell gazed at the images of two young girls standing in a meadow near a woods. Diaphanous wings seemed to protrude from the girls' shoulders.

John Darnell looked quizzically at Doyle, waiting for his explanation. And Penny's lips silently formed a word she hadn't used seriously since primary school.

Sir Arthur Conan Doyle smiled darkly. He said simply the word on Penny's lips to which she had given no sound. "Fairies."

Chapter 30

Monday, December 25, 1916

Sung smiled at Ho San, who held a silver platter and looked at his father expectantly. "Place goose in center of table, son. That's right."

Ho San beamed as he placed the silver dish on the table, between the two silver candlesticks. Lamps burned dimly in corners of the dining room, and the flickering candles gave a soft glow to the table and the room. Darnell sat at one end of the table and Penny at the other. Two other places were set on opposite sides of the table.

"You are sure we eat with you here? Could eat in kitchen." Sung's forehead wrinkled with the question.

"Of course, you'll sit here," Darnell said. "We talked that all through last night, Sung. It's Christmas! Now, take your seats. When we need something, well, we'll just get up and get it."

Penny said, "After cooking such a perfect goose, Sung, you're entitled to share in it."

Ho San took a seat and looked from Darnell to Penny with anticipation. "First time we are having Christmas dinner with you. We thank you."

"First, but not last," Darnell said. "Now, Sung, just pour the wine and we'll carve that bird."

Sung complied, pouring the red Bordeaux in glasses for the two of them. "I do not drink," he said.

"I know," Darnell said. "But you do eat." He stood over the bird with knife and fork. He carved off the legs and wings and placed them on a platter, then addressed the breast with the sharp knife, making precise slices and transferring them to the dish, beside the other pieces. He handed the platter to Sung. "Help yourself and pass it. That's American style."

Penny laughed. "You've got a good memory, John."

He lifted his glass and reached over to hers, touching it gently, a musical sound resulting. "Here's to all of us. Merry Christmas!" Darnell sipped his wine and watched as the others prepared their plates, then he filled his own.

"This goose," Penny said to Sung, "is just wonderful. You have a way with cooking it."

He smiled. "Chinese secret. I teach Ho San, too. He watches me cook."

The boy's expression was serious as he looked at his father. "I could never cook like Father."

They talked as they ate, and it was soon time for dessert. Sung and Ho San cleared the table, and Sung returned with the plum pudding he had promised to prepare. "Customary to put trinkets in plum pudding. There are four."

"Then we'd better look for them before we break our teeth," Darnell said.

"I have one! A ring." Penny held it up for Darnell to see. "That's good luck."

"And I have a coin," Ho San said. He looked at it closely. "It's a shilling."

"Not just shilling," Sung said. "*New* shilling. Never used. Direct from bank."

"Another ring," Darnell said. "You know, Penny, I think Sung planned it this way."

Penny laughed, and looked at Sung. "Your turn, Sung. Let's see what you have."

Sung poked at his pudding with a fork and found his prize. He held it out on his fork. "A thimble. Need it to darn socks."

"Very practical, Sung." Darnell sampled the pudding. "And your dessert is excellent. Tasty, indeed."

Darnell looked about the table with contentment. The case was over. Only one thing remained—he'd see Sandy MacDougall to tell him as much of the story as he felt should reach the pages of *The Times,* and insist the rest be withheld. The Prime Minister needed no adverse publicity to cloud his conduct of the war. Sandy would understand that.

Darnell said to Sung, "Penny and I will have our coffee by the Christmas tree." He took Penny's arm and the two walked across the entry into the sitting room, warm with the fire from the hearth and dimly lit with several candles.

The Christmas tree, standing in the corner, laden with ornaments, sparkled in the flickering firelight and candlelight, and the two darkened silhouettes of John and Penny Darnell blended into one as he took her in his arms and they stood admiring the tree. In a moment, they sat on the sofa and quietly watched the fire dancing.

"John," Penny said with some hesitation. "There's something I wonder about, something a bit sensitive."

"Yes?" He looked into her eyes, wondering.

"Have you . . . come to an end in your search for Jeffrey?"

"My search?"

"I know something passed between you and Madame Ispenska last night, from the few words I overheard."

Darnell took a deep breath. She had broached it, and now he could tell her. He described the midnight séance at Madame Ispenska's house, how it bothered him, how he wondered what was true and what was not. "Last night she told me she'd overheard me talking about Jeff with Conan Doyle at the second séance."

"So she knew about Jeffrey, and pretended . . . ?"

"No, she didn't say that." He frowned. "She believes in her powers. She was only trying to give me a way out, a reason *not to believe* what happened, if I chose not to."

Penny took his hands in hers. "John, I think through all of this, part of you wanted the séances to be real, wanted the voices to be real, so you could hear Jeffrey's voice again, even though it was against all your instincts. It must have been a great conflict."

Darnell sighed. "Those thoughts or desires may have flickered in and out of my mind. But in the end, I knew it couldn't be true. I questioned everything Madame Ispenska did. Yes, I may have wished for it to be true, but all that happened was that I learned the strength of my own beliefs." He paused. "I know I can never reach Jeffrey, as my mother wanted to do, years ago. But he'll always be with me. In memories and dreams. And at every Christmas, the time of year that Jeffrey loved so much, when I think of him, I'll know he'll be forever a child, seven years old."

Darnell held Penny close as he talked. She'd helped him, as she always did when he needed her. In a husky voice, he said, "Let's go up, Penny. I can wait until morning for coffee, but right now, I want to be alone with you."

Penny smiled. "Yes, John. The case is over. We deserve some time together. For our own private séance."